Advance praise for
Gallows Hill

"Set against the hysteria of the Salem witch trials, this richly
detailed novel is both immersive and timely. The two young
narrators wrestle with questions of faith, gender, and justice—
and how much to risk for those they love."

—Susan Kaplan Carlton, author of *In the Neighborhood of*

"Through the eyes of her flawed but persevering fictional
characters, Lois Ruby paints a vivid picture of prejudice,
suspicion, and the cruelty that results from them."

—Mary Downing Hahn, author of *What W*

"Ruby has crafted a gripping and harrowing account of one of
darkest chapters in American history, a time when people tur
on family, friends, and neighbors. Told in crisp and vivid det
Gallows Hill brings history to life for readers young and old."

—Carolee Dean, author of *Forget*

"Rich in telling detail, *Gallows Hill* brings the world of 1692
Massachusetts, to vivid life. While spinning a page-turner
satisfying story, author Lois Ruby allows the past to speak t
now in the clear voices of Thomas and Patience, an appeali
pair of teenagers caught up in a tumultuous time of widespr
misinformation and mass hysteria, who have the courage to
for themselves and question everything. Highly recommen

—Sandra Fenichel Asher, author and pla

GALLOWS HILL

Lois Ruby

carolrhoda LAB
MINNEAPOLIS

Carolrhoda Lab®
An imprint of Lerner Publishing Group, Inc.
241 First Avenue North
Minneapolis, MN 55401 USA

For reading levels and more information, look up this title at www.lernerbooks.com.

Images used: Stephanie Frey/Shutterstock; Bruce Rolff/Shutterstock; Slava Gerj/Shutterstock;
Damien Che/Shutterstock; Alfmaler/Shutterstock.

Main body text set in Janson Text LT Std. Typeface provided by Adobe Systems.

Library of Congress Cataloging-in-Publication Data

Names: Ruby, Lois, author.
Title: Gallows Hill / Lois Ruby.
Description: Minneapolis, MN : Carolrhoda Lab, [2023] | Audience: Ages 11–18. | Audience:
    Grades 10–12. | Summary: Told in alternating voices, in 1692 Salem, Puritan Patience
    and Quaker Thomas are engrossed in a community panic over witchcraft, and as the list of
    accusers and accused grows, they question their faiths and fight to protect their families.
Identifiers: LCCN 2022045264 (print) | LCCN 2022045265 (ebook) | ISBN 9781728431024 |
    ISBN 9781728493947 (ebook)
Subjects: CYAC: Witchcraft—Fiction. | Trials (Witchcraft)—Fiction. | Salem (Mass.)—
    History—Colonial period, ca. 1600–1775—Fiction. | LCGFT: Historical fiction. | Novels.
Classification: LCC PZ7.R8314 Gal 2023 (print) | LCC PZ7.R8314 (ebook) | DDC [Fic]—dc23

LC record available at https://lccn.loc.gov/2022045264
LC ebook record available at https://lccn.loc.gov/2022045265

Manufactured in the United States of America
1-49524-49540-1/18/2023

For Aunt Dodo,
Dorothy Ruby Saxe,
who never judged a soul

Chapter 1
Late February 1692

Thomas

"Come quick, boy!" One of the sailors on deck beckons to me. "Your father, he's turned real bad. Your sister's down there with 'im, but 'e's calling for you."

I drag myself away from the rail of the ship. What little I've eaten has already landed in the ocean as supper for the whales. I wipe my mouth on my sleeve as the icy wind whips and tears at the sails. North wind? East wind? Impossible to tell, as howling torrents and gusts slam my face from every direction and frosty seawater laps at my back.

The ship lurches like a drunken sailor, and Heaven knows there are plenty of that kind aboard. The short walk across the deck forces me to climb uphill, then plummet downhill, and my stomach rises and falls with the waves.

I am not seaworthy.

Down below, Father lies on his thin mattress of straw, from which he hasn't moved in two days. Other voyagers fill the dark, airless cabin, swaying with the thrusting water. Each of us has carved out our own precious inches to ourselves. Mine is at the foot of Father's cot, when I'm not up on the top deck retching.

Father's eyes flutter open when he smells me nearby. Grace, my sister, moves aside to make way, shaking out the filthy rag she's been using to wipe Father's face. Yesterday was her thirteenth birthday and tomorrow will be my fifteenth, without us sparing much thought for either.

Father's thin voice beckons me closer: "My son, does thee hear me?"

"Yes, Father."

"Look behind me. See? Thy mother stands there, with sweet baby Matilde clutched to her heart."

If only Mother *were* here. Already I fear I'm forgetting her face. And I never set eyes on the infant Matilde, whose Inner Light never shone. She returned to our Creator with Mother.

Father's labored words grow more urgent. "Does thee see them?"

I glance at Grace, rooted to the floor where seawater has seeped in through the wooden slats. Her eyes are ringed with red. "Yes, Father," we murmur together, although there is no woman or baby behind him.

Father's hand rests on my arm. "Thy mother and sister have come to take me with them. I shall not live to see another sunrise."

"You—*thee* must not say that!" In the five weeks we've been crossing the Atlantic, we've been ridiculed often for our *thee*s and *thy*s, which mark us for members of the Religious Society of Friends. Our fellow passengers sneer at us, call us Quakers, remind us that only a few decades ago we were outlawed among the Puritans of the Massachusetts Bay Colony as well as by the Church of England. To keep the taunts at bay, Grace and I have resorted to the worldly *you* when Father is out of hearing range.

Father's raspy whisper pulls me closer to him. "Son, when the ship docks at Salem, thee must find thy way to Eberly the shipwright." His eyes swim in his head for a moment before they snap wider to search my face. "Tell Goodman Eberly I cannot come to work with him as promised. In my place thee must apprentice thyself to him . . . learn our trade . . . else thee and Grace shall not survive."

Apprentice myself? But I aim to continue school, to read law. The Bay Colony has a fine university, so we've heard. Words swarm like music in my soul, like the plucked strings of a forbidden lute. I have no wish to build ships. If I live long enough to get to New England—and nearly half the people we began the voyage with have already died—I hope never to see another ship for the rest of my life.

Father reaches out and pulls my ear to his cracked lips. "Thee must take care of thy sister. Before sundown, my body shall slide into the sea. Thee must not let thy sister witness it. Promise me . . ."

No other words come from Father's lips.

Patience

Life long, I have tried to live up to my name, but I have missed the mark a thousand times. Ask anyone. I am never patient. Sunrise cannot come soon enough for me. In winter I yearn for spring, and in spring I hunger for summer's corn and wild cranberries that bring such zest to Mother's occasional roast of venison. During the endless hours in the meetinghouse on the Lord's Day, I itch to be outside and on my feet, but during the week I dream of rest.

Father is a fisherman, and Mother is the finest fishmonger in the market square. My younger sister, Abigail, and I stand in awe of her as her patter draws crowds to our stall: "Codfish, fruit of the Bay; codfish, fruit of the Bay." To Mother's left, candlemaker Goody Simms sings out, "Beeswax, tallow, bayberry. Very merry bayberry!" All the while, Goodman Cade, the carpenter, drums the rhythm of their song with nails pounded into wood.

Their voices weave in and out of one another's almost like music, but of course we faithful saints do not indulge in music outside of psalms, and our odd Quaker neighbors not even that much. The Catholics? Well, they're a raucous bunch! So I've heard, at least.

I admit I've been known to sing psalms under my breath at the market. Mother's nosy friend, Goodwife Mulberry, once caught me in song with my mouth gaping wide, as if I were a nestling awaiting a fat, tasty worm. The goodwife demanded that I recite a dozen times a verse from Psalm 119—*Lord, do not let me be put to shame*—and stood there the whole while, counting off.

And here comes Goodwife Mulberry now, brimming with gossip for Mother. No doubt she brings news of the afflicted girls—Reverend Parris's daughter and niece, Goodman Putnam's daughter, and Dr. Griggs's niece. For weeks now they've been writhing in pain, swearing that some unseen villain is pinching them mercilessly. Unexplainable bouts of blindness, deafness, dizziness, and feverish whirling plague them. Some say their arms are twisted clear out of their sockets. That I have not seen, myself.

Dr. Griggs has declared the girls bewitched, but both he and Reverend Parris have been at a loss to find either a cure or a culprit. There's prayer, of course, and other methods, including live toads baked and burned and pounded into a black powder for tea. Pity those toads! And then there was the witch-cake. We've heard that Goodwife Sibley had Reverend Parris's servants, Tituba and her husband, collect the water of the afflicted girls and bake it with ground meal. The cake was fed to a dog, poor thing, and that was supposed to cause the girls' tormentor to come forth. It did not work, but the dog survived unscathed. I'm glad our Ruff wasn't the one to taste that putrid cake.

"Goodwife Woodstock, have you heard?" asks Goodwife Mulberry, out of breath. "The girls have named their tormentors! One is Tituba, Reverend Parris's servant. The other two are Sarah Osborne and Sarah Good. Witches, all!"

This is news indeed. Tituba should be no surprise, I suppose, being from Barbados. We Christians have been taught that Indians worship the Devil. Though I've heard that Tituba knows our Scripture well—perhaps because she's been so long enslaved to a minister? As for the others . . .

"Sarah Good!" gasps Abigail beside me.

Of course Goodwife Mulberry hears her. "Is she not your neighbor these days?"

Mother snorts. "Barely a neighbor in fact, and certainly not one in spirit."

Our garden backs against the shabby hovel where William and Sarah Good stay with their sweet daughter, Dorothy. Mother says William Good is shiftless. He deserted his wife and daughter in Salem Town until they had no roof over their heads and barely a heel of bread for their stomachs. They came here to Salem Village, begging and borrowing, shuffling from field to field and barn to barn, until they moved into the eyesore hut behind us.

Abigail and I sometimes chortle about how she's called Goody Good, when in fact she's sour and fierce-tempered, always shouting at somebody or else muttering curses under her breath. But a witch! I never suspected it. And for all her parents' sins and troubles, little Dorothy, only four years old, is as gentle-tempered a child as I ever met. From time to time I'll look after the little girl while Sarah Good goes out to beg. Most days she's fortunate to come by a rotting chicken leg or a handful of cornmeal for porridge. Abigail and I slip Dorothy bits of bread and garden vegetables when we can manage it.

Goodwife Mulberry's lip curls in contempt as she talks of Sarah Good. "Not a member of our congregation, not a land-owner's wife, not . . . well, not *anything*, that one. And her scoun-drel husband, he's no better. For too long those wretches have gone from house to house begging for food and money. And when virtuous, upstanding citizens—such as we are, Goody Woodstock—when we denied her, she muttered curses under her breath. Foul breath, I might add."

Most days, Mother would clamp her hands over both my ears rather than allow me to hear such sinful gossip, for the psalms tell us, *Set a guard, O Lord, over my mouth; keep watch over the door of my lips.* I confess, my door swings open now and then. But even good people prattle on in times like these. In fact, gossip has become the local currency, as prized as coin, as prized as fresh meat.

Goodwife Mulberry rushes on. "And now young Elizabeth Hubbard"—that's Dr. Griggs's niece—"has said she was fol-lowed home the other night by a wolf and that this beast is Sarah Good's familiar. I expect we'll soon learn all her dark deeds. There'll be warrants for the witches' arrest, and the town fathers will see to it that they're punished for the harm they've done those poor girls."

Abigail tugs on my sleeve. She's twelve, nearly three years younger than I, but far prettier with her hair so dark and curly, her eyes a luminous gray. I am plain—brown hair, eyes the faded green of late-summer leaves, oatmeal-hued skin that blotches red in the sunlight.

"Look!" says Abigail. She draws her skirt up from her ankle to show us welts that redden her legs. "I'm afflicted too. Just like the other girls!"

"Those look like mosquito bites to me," I say.

Her eyes drill into mine. "Mosquitoes in winter? Nonsense!"

My sister has always had a lively imagination. Perhaps it comes of all the reading she does. We are each taught to read, of course—else how would we know the Bible? But some make sense of those squiggles with more, well, *joy* than others do. I've only ever mastered enough to read a psalm or two, as any of God's children should.

Abigail says, "An evil witch afflicted me so, and I know who it was!"

Mother slaps down a mackerel and huffs, "You say a witch is plaguing you, at the precise time when I happen to need your help earning our daily bread? Come now, child!"

But Abigail draws up her shift as far as her petticoat and displays the red blotches to us all—even old Goodman Cade, whose eyes are as big as peonies at the sight of so much feminine limb.

"It's Sarah Good, I tell you!" Abigail is nearly yelling now. "Sarah Good is the witch who's done this to me!"

Chapter 2
February

Thomas

The rich people from the upper decks saunter down the gang-plank in fancy dress they've saved for this very moment. We of the lower decks stumble off the ship, filthy and exhausted, half-blinded by the unexpected sunlight as a blast of frosty air assaults us. Some of us are barely alive, but we are here, in New England.

Passengers scatter to waiting family. Three ladies on our deck have come to be matched with husbands they've never met. Everyone has someplace to go except Grace and me. We're alone.

The wharf is crowded with residents hurrying here and there, most wearing humble linen and wool. We're scruffy after our weeks on the ship, but the Salem folk take no notice of us amid the hogs and chickens and goats and sows saun-tering through the town. The smell is horrid and at the same time intoxicating: rotting vegetables, unwashed bodies, horse manure, salt-water fish, and smoke rising from nearby chim-neys promising warmth and roasted meat. We haven't tasted meat in months. I've no idea where we'll come by a morsel to fill our stomachs, which are inside-out with hunger.

I pull Grace along toward a craggy man perched on a rock. "Pardon me, sir, but can you tell me where I might find Eberly the shipwright?"

The man claps me on the shoulder. "I'm no *sir*, boy. Sirs are the landed gentry, or at least the rich, like that fine fellow yonder with the fancy boot buckles. Sawtucket, at yer service." He doffs his hat and bows broadly like a man I once saw in a street performance, acting the part of a court jester. Though we Friends hold that all theater is deceitful and therefore sinful, Father let me tarry a few moments to watch the spectacle.

Father. Gone from us. A wave of grief washes through me again.

"Pleased to meet you, Goodman Sawtucket"—for that's how to address the next caste of New Englanders properly.

"No *goodman*, neither. Just Sawtucket."

"Sawtucket, can you kindly direct us to Eberly?"

"Hmm." He thrusts his palm toward me and flexes his fingers in a come-forth way.

Am I to pay him in exchange for information about the shipbuilder? I pluck a coin out of my pocket. There are so few.

"Dead in the water," Sawtucket says, snapping his stubby fingers around the coin. "That's life on ye. Shipbuilder, dead in the water. Yes, me boy, he went down with one of his faulty boats. Look for him at the bottom of the bay."

Grace stares at Sawtucket. "But he's our last hope, Eberly is. There's no one else, and we're orphans."

"Sawtucket," I say, "do you know of any other Friends— Quakers like ourselves—who might take us in?"

"Few enough Quakers hereabouts, fewer still could afford to feed two more mouths—and with suspicion already on their heads?" He clucks his tongue. "Best steer clear of Quakers. Time was, not long ago, they'd be run out of Salem or hanged as heretics."

"We are no such thing!" Grace snaps.

He squints one eye at us. "Or witches."

I aim to answer steadily, convincingly. "I can promise none of us dabble in witchcraft."

Sawtucket shrugs. "Still, just now, that's all anyone can talk about—aye, who's a witch and who's bewitched by a witch. The parson's daughter and niece were the first touched, back in January, and now two more girls. All tormented by the Devil's servants, folk say." He slaps his hand to his chest. "Others say it, not me."

Tears spring to Grace's blue eyes, and I say firmly, "Never mind, sister. We have each other."

"If ye're lookin' for a home," says Sawtucket, "I may know a good place for ye to lay your heads." The palm flattens again, and Grace motions for me to dig out another coin.

"That all ye got?"

"Not a ha'penny more," I say stoutly.

He grunts. "So, there's a sweet old widow, Prudence Blevins—bad with the rheumatism, barren as a mule, slightly daft, and in need of young'uns to look after her, fetch wood and such."

Grace brightens. "Is she a good woman, sir? She won't beat us, will she?"

"Shouldn't think so, frail as she is these days. And she'll have no fear to take ye in. Fears nothing, that one."

I say, "Kindly tell us where to find her."

"Easy as pigeon pie. She's just over in Salem Village."

Confused, I ask, "Then where are we now?"

"Salem Town, the one with the harbor. A mile or two northwest's the Village, what folks used to call the Farms 'cause it's mostly pasture, with its few hundred souls hankering to be something they're not." He chuckles to himself. "They're right proud to have their own meetinghouse and minister, but 'twas the minister's own daughter and niece was the first afflicted. The Devil come right there into the house of the good Reverend Samuel Parris, can ye top that?"

He gives us directions to the home of Goodwidow Blevins, and though his palm is out again, I choose not to reward it. Grace is already tugging at my coat.

"Mind ye now," Sawtucket calls after us, "the old widow has a bit of a reputation, both here in Salem Town and in Salem Village yonder."

"A reputation for what?" I ask, wary now.

Sawtucket licks his lips and runs his tongue over his few teeth before he says, "That one? She's a witch."

Grace gasps. "Then why send us to her?"

Sawtucket shrugs. "I know for a fact she's got room for ye."

"Come, Grace," I say. "We'll see if this goodwidow will take us in for a night or two, until we can sort ourselves out." I'm hurrying her helter-skelter down the lane before Sawtucket can say more to unsettle us. But his words ring in my ears.

We wander like lost hounds along unfamiliar lanes, asking a few goodwives for directions until we've walked miles, carrying our bundles, and roundabout end up at a hut with a thatched roof, surrounded by a garden whose weeds choke the few shriveled carrots left rotting in the dirt from last summer.

Grace tilts her head—always a dangerous sign, because it means she's hatching a plan. "I could help with the garden."

Pointing to the door that hangs askew from bent hinges, I mutter, "This place needs far more than gardening." Two splintery steps lead to the door, bits of the gray wood crumbling under our feet. I knock with more confidence than I feel.

A walnut-wrinkled face leans out the window. "I don't want none! Go away! If you don't scuttle off, I'll take my axe to your heads quick as a whistle and use you for kindling."

Patience

With Abigail too agitated to be of any use at the market, Mother has sent us home to attend to our other chores. On account of her delicate stomach, Abigail will be the lucky one to breathe in the delicious frosty air—feeding our geese, sweeping our doorstep, and digging up leeks and radishes in our winter garden. Which delivers me to the vile work of emptying and scouring the chamber pots—ugh!—and tending the fire to cook our noon fish stew.

And yet *she's* the one of us who's grumbling—still going on about her afflictions. She never used to be so fretful, but ever since those girls fell ill last month and there's been talk of the Devil's servants causing it, she's been out of sorts.

"Perhaps I should go for Dr. Griggs," I say, to needle her. "And you can explain to Father why we must pay his fee."

Abigail's eyes go wide. "No! Not the doctor. He'll set those revolting leeches on me or give me a rope of wolf fangs to hang around my neck. Neither one will cure me, and Father will say it's money ill spent."

"Shall we take you to Reverend Parris, then? He can pray over you."

"Him? Father can barely abide him," Abigail huffs.

To be honest, I'm not fond of our minister either. He seems a bit arrogant for a modest man of the cloth, and he does rant on and on about how the flock is under the thumb of the Devil. I should think it would be his job to keep Satan *out* of our congregation. Odd, isn't it, that it's Reverend Parris's daughter and niece who were first afflicted? Is there something amiss in the minister's house that drew the Devil there? The prospect thrills me. Oh, it shouldn't.

Done with my other chores, I take up knitting a webbed weir for Father to catch fish in, come spring. But the moment I've begun to work, I hear shouts coming from the shack behind our house. William Good must have deigned to visit his wife. I would never stoop to gossip, but truthfully, husband and wife argue day and night, loudly. She'll say, *You're a drunk, a good-for-nothing louse!* And he'll say, *You're a witch of a wench if ever I saw one, handmaiden of Satan himself!* And the curses that issue from her mouth! That foul language alone condemns her as a sinner. As Mother likes to say, the more you stir it, the worse it stinks.

Oh, it's ugly business between them, and I have to lean out the window to catch every word.

A large black crow clings to a bare branch and tilts his head toward the Goods' hut as if he's listening as well. What tales will he take to the rest of the flock?

But now, the man's voice I hear is not William Good's. I venture outside for a better look and see our constable, Goodman Herrick, binding Sarah Good's hands with thick rope.

Goodwife Sarah Good is being arrested!

She spits and kicks as Goodman Herrick jerks her up the lane. Her eyes are wild, shot with blood, and her hair pops out of her bonnet—left, right, top and bottom.

Voice pounding the air, she yells over her shoulder, "Patience Woodstock! Look after my baby. Her scoundrel father's nowhere to be found, and my Dorothy is all alone."

I duck back into my house for fear the constable will think me an accomplice in Goody Good's devilish work.

But once they've gone, I slip into the Goods' shack to rescue poor little Dorothy.

She sits trembling by the door. "Ma-a-a-a," she wails, and my heart cleaves in two.

I wrap my arms around her, and she collapses against me.

We can't leave her on her own to freeze and starve in this horrid hut. And who but we Woodstocks would take her in? Abigail and I have room up in our loft, so little Dorothy can sleep across our feet. I might have to keep her scarce when Father is awake, but soon enough she'll fit right in like Ruff, and he'll barely notice. He barely notices *us* except when he reads the Bible to us in the evenings.

After a moment she pulls away from me, suddenly calmed. "There he is," she says sweetly.

"Who, Dorothy? Where?"

"There. Under the chair where Mama sits and sews."

Is the child deranged with hunger? Lifting the chair, I show her that there's nothing under it.

"Oh, he's slithered away. He hides from me sometimes."

"Who?"

"The snake. The one who talks to me and sucks blood from my thumb."

Chapter 3
February

Thomas

"Use us for kindling, will she?" Grace huffs.

"I'll find us another place to live," I assure her, though I have no idea where.

"This one suits me well enough." Grace pounds on the lopsided door. No one comes to answer it, but the latch doesn't hold—if indeed there is a latch—and under pressure the door swings open a bit. Grace marches straight in before I can stop her, stepping over the rubbish strewn on the floor and sniffing the stale air.

"Thomas, I believe the goodwidow's mother did not teach her about welcoming strangers. As it says in the Book, *Do not neglect to show hospitality to strangers, for thereby some have entertained angels unawares.*"

When has Grace become so angelic?

The old woman shuffles toward us and squints to see more clearly, doubtless wondering who could be so brash as my young sister.

Grace sidesteps her and moves to the table, inspecting a wooden plate encrusted with days-old crumbs and a pewter tankard that's growing mold. "Thomas, would thee agree that help is needed here?" She whips up the patchwork blanket on the old woman's bed of straw. Snapping it a good time or two, which raises mighty clouds of dust, she lays the blanket smartly on the bed and turns to the astonished old woman.

"My brother and I are hard workers. All we need, kind goodwidow, is a bit of bread. Soon, I might add. And porridge in the morning. Also a spot to spread out our bedrolls." She spins about. "Yes, that corner will do nicely, once it's swept."

Grace takes up a ragged straw broom and begins sweeping.

Wide-eyed, Goodwidow Blevins drops into the one chair in the room. "What gives you the right to . . . ?"

But Grace merely lifts the widow's feet, shoed in holey leather, to sweep beneath them. "Right, indeed! It's clear that *someone* must take matters in hand here. Thomas, can thee just imagine what it must be like in the privy outside?" Brazen and spiky—so like our mother, God rest her.

The old woman shakes her head. "What am I to do with the both of you ragamuffins?"

Well, she hasn't welcomed us into her hut, but neither has she chased us away.

Patience

I've brought Dorothy to our house, and I neglect the afternoon's chores to tend to her, settling her on the bench with an old cloth doll. At times she seems content, but every so often she still cries for her mother.

Abigail comes in from our winter garden with the day's harvest. "Why's the child blathering so? She's lucky to be rid of that woman. A plague to everybody even before we knew she was a witch! Sneaks barefooted into people's bedrooms when they're fast asleep. Pinches children, even babies! Threatens and puts curses on anyone she dislikes, and right afterward their cows die!"

Dorothy jams her face into my stomach, and I clap my hands over her ears. "Don't say such things, not in front of the poor child."

"But we know even worse of her now!" Abigail's mouth twists into a grimace. "Sarah Good is covenanted with Satan himself."

"Sister! Hush. Whatever Goodwife Good's sins, Dorothy has no one to care for her but her mother."

Dorothy says, "And the man with the black hat. I saw him last night. He took me out of Mama's arms and gave me a sweet. He is as kind a man as can be."

Suddenly Abigail begins to whirl, grasping her head as if to keep it from exploding. Dorothy turns around to stare, and it's as though a bolt of lightning runs between the two of them. Abigail seizes, sinks to the floor, her face poppy red. She's gasping for breath. "Get her off of me! Sarah Good—I can't breathe with the weight of her on me!"

"But sister, you know Goody Good's been arrested."

"No! She's here. I can't breathe!" Suddenly her body stiffens, and I'm terrified that she's passed on to the next world! But no, her eyes dart about. They're glassy and seem to be looking inward, not at me.

I try to lift Abigail, but she is suddenly the weight of three men. I cannot budge her. Meanwhile Dorothy is muttering something, a chant of some sort. She bites the eyes off the doll and tosses it at Abigail.

My sister slowly sits upright, blinking, and asks, "What happened, Patience? I had a frightful nightmare." She suddenly jabs a finger in Dorothy's direction. "You! You were in it."

Dorothy sits with a curious smile spread across her angelic face.

Chapter 4
February

Thomas

Seeing that Grace has things well in hand, I go out in search of work. I shyly stop several men, asking, "Sir, have you the name of a shipwright?" Any shipwright will do so I can earn a few pennies. Shipbuilding is possibly the last trade on earth I'd care to learn, but I know even less of other crafts.

Men frown and glare at me, and it occurs to me that they're put off by my clothing, which is dirty and no doubt foul smelling, but also the garb of a member of the Society of Friends. My flat-brimmed hat alone signals that I am not a Puritan. Finally, a man waves me toward the premises of Goodman Murdock.

I find him shaping wood for the keel of an enormous boat. I have yet to grasp the difference between a large boat and a small ship.

"Goodman, I've come seeking work."

"You know the craft, do you?"

"No, sir. But my father did."

"And you apprenticed to him?"

I hang my head. "No, sir."

He notches two thick boards to make a curve. "As a boy, this is all I dreamed of doing, building a sturdy watertight boat and sailing away to the other side of the world. Are you like me?"

"No, sir. I had a keen mind for my studies, and my father let me keep at them." This isn't going well, or maybe it is. Half my soul hopes he takes me on immediately, for Grace and I have nothing to live on and Goodwidow Blevins hasn't much more herself. The other half hopes he'll send me away.

His voice grows cross. "So, why have you come to me, boy?" He tugs at the two thick boards he's notched to see that they're fixed tight, and they are, like a hand in a glove.

What shall I tell him but a near-truth? "Goodman Eberly sent me, sir, before his untimely death."

Goodman Murdock looks up sharply, waving some sort of angled, pointed tool toward me. "Gone to meet his Maker, poor sot. Best shipwright around New England, after meself. Well, if my jovial rival sent you, I suppose I ought to give you a chance. Know what this is, boy?" He holds the tool up under my nose. If his hand were to slip, my nose would be sliced off clean.

Cupping my nose, I venture: "A . . . chisel? A . . . borer?"

"Neither—a raze. Know what kind of wood I'm working here?" He strokes it lovingly, the way you'd pet a cat at your feet.

"Pine? Maple?"

Goodman Murdock throws his head back and laughs, flashing picket-fence teeth. "Oak, son, oak. You have much to learn. Whatever did Eberly see in you?" He grows pensive. "Have you a place to live, a roof over your head?"

"My sister and I stay with Goodwidow Blevins for now, sir."

The shipwright lifts both eyebrows, bushy as squirrel tails. "I suppose you're too freshly arrived to know anything of the goings-on here. There are girls, much like your sister, beset with strange afflictions no one can explain."

"You don't know my sister, sir. She's unshakable solid as . . . oak. She's taken the woman in hand. Anyway, who else but Goodwidow Blevins would take in such an opinionated wench and her brother, a shipbuilder of great promise?"

He chuckles again but sobers quickly. "Beware, son. There are three women already accused of witchcraft, and they may not be the last."

"I've heard the rumor, sir, that the widow is a witch. She seems harmless enough to us."

"Aye, but only the Lord in Heaven knows for sure."

I shift from foot to foot. "We'll not stay there long, sir. Only until we can find better accommodations." Though I'm not sure I believe this myself, now that Grace has resolved to carve out a place for us in the widow's hut.

"Well," says Goodman Murdock, "it'd be too much of a risk to take you on for seven years' indenture straightaway. But I can pay you two pennies a day until you learn enough to earn your keep. Then we shall talk."

Patience

Our table is usually as silent as a Quaker meeting. Father returns from the morning's ice fishing as ravenous as a bear, and the only sound at our noonday meal is him slurping his fish soup. Abigail and I stand behind him, as proper daughters do, with tiny Dorothy nearly hidden in my skirt, and our dog, Ruff, waiting for a morsel to drop to the floor. We're to be focusing our thoughts on the bounty of good food—fresh fish, salted fish, and more of it—that God has provided for us. To spend the energy welling up in me, or else I'd burst, I'm tapping my toes.

Perhaps a different name would've suited me better. Charity? That seems boastful. Temperance? So hard to maintain, and certainly not Diligence, which sounds like drudgery. Humility, perhaps—there is a name I could carry proudly.

Suddenly Father slashes the silence with some news: "Hathorne and Corwin are examining the witches tomorrow morning at Ingersoll's. There's talk that those three hags will hang."

My foot stops in midair. Mother sucks a piece of potato out of her teeth and inspects it. "No tooth in it, thank the Lord," she murmurs to herself.

"Goodman Cade, he's been picked to build the gallows," Father goes on, as calmly as if he were talking about fish scales. "Out at the west edge of town, that hill out there."

"There'll be no talk of hanging at my table, hear?" says Mother. She casts an eye toward the child peeking out from behind my skirt.

Father follows her gaze and scowls. "When's William Good coming to collect *that*?"

"Lord knows," Mother says. "I expect he'll abandon the pitiful little one. Word is, he has no heart for his wife—less than he did before, now that she's been arrested."

"What man in his right mind abides holy matrimony with a witch?" Father says.

I clasp both arms around Dorothy as Father, bless his heart, carries on. There's no hope of stopping him when he gets up some speed.

"That child is just as bad, no doubt. Runs in families, through the mother, witchcraft does."

"Like brown hair or big feet?" I wiggle my toes, and yes, my feet are ungainly and large, though Mother's are tiny.

Father turns and glowers at me. "Watch your saucy mouth, daughter."

My tongue always does work faster than my brain. I know better than to cross him—the head of our house, the closest to God among us—and I shrink at his sharp tone.

Abigail's eyes find mine, and for a change I see sympathy in them.

Mother clears her throat but says nothing more. Soon she'll go back to her stall in the market square with Father's latest catch, and Father will snore through the rest of the afternoon, since he's up three hours before the cock crows to dig through the ice and wake the fish. We'll all breathe easier once he's at rest. Though I can't erase from my mind's eye the image of that gallows going up on the hill.

Suddenly Abigail rears back and slams against the wall, as if battered by a gust of wind off the sea. "Yeow! Stop pinching me!"

"Be still, daughter," Father commands, and she tries, but it's as though something, someone, is yanking her about. Obviously the strong-smelling bag of asafetida that Mother fixed around Abigail's neck is not working its cure.

"Do you not see her?" Abigail jabs her finger at the air. "Sarah Good. She's right there."

None but the five of us here, plus Ruff.

"Abigail," Mother says, straining to stay calm, though her nostrils are flaring, "you know very well that Goodwife Good is locked up."

"No! She's here. See?"

"Mama's here?" Dorothy asks.

Abigail points. "See? She's floating above me now, up in the rafters. Hear her laughing at me?"

Father shoves his soup aside and pulls Abigail down to the bench, his hand pressing into her shoulder. "If the wicked Sarah Good has been hooked into the net of the Old Deluder—if she's doing these ungodly things to you, daughter—then I swear, I will personally see that she's the first one led to the gallows."

Thomas

"No, no, lad!" shouts Goodman Murdock's saw gang leader as I point to a slab of wood. "Too rigid to be shaped into the keel of a ship. Nay, not that one either. Look, it's too pocked with squirrel holes to ever make for a watertight ship. Get out. You've no eye for wood."

So I'm put to steaming the stiff oak timbers until they can bend a bit. But soon enough I over-steam my plank so that it's bowed out of shape and unfit for anything but kindling, and even then only when it dries out in a month or two. I'm sent back to Goodman Murdock.

"All right," he says with a weary sigh. "Wood is not your element. Let us see how you do in the sail loft. Can you stitch, son?"

Not well enough, it seems, to avoid poking holes in my fingers and bleeding all over the flax. And after my first try at twisting hemp, the ropemaker shoves me against the wall. "You lubberwort! You clapperdudgeon!"

I stumble back to Goodman Murdock, who shakes his head in disbelief. He's heard that I'm a lubberwort and a clapperdudgeon. Which is worse?

Goodman Murdock rattles the money pouch around his waist and fishes out some coins. "I shall give you your promised two for today. The Good Book says a man should receive his wages after a day's work. And I shall give you two more pennies if you swear never to return to shipbuilding for all eternity."

I'm awash in relief, greedily eyeing the four coins.

"Cordwaining—I believe that's your calling, son." He nods toward my scuffed shoes.

I've never fancied myself a shoemaker, but surely it can't be worse than shipbuilding.

"Go to the cordwainer on Front Street. Cawley's his name. Makes new shoes and mends old ones too. He's a gruff bear, but there's a heart deep inside all that flesh. Ask anybody in Salem, town or village—they'd vouch for his character. He's due back from a trip to Boston next Monday. Best not to tell him I sent you, in case your talent for leather and nails rivals your talent for lumber and sails." His eyes twinkle as he warms my hand with four pence.

Grace and I are rich!

"By the bye," adds Goodman Murdock, "you say you've attended to your studies. Can you write? I've heard that the magistrates Hathorne and Corwin are conducting an examination of three accused witches tomorrow at Ingersoll's inn."

"Is writing evidence of witchcraft?" I mean it as a jest, though I wonder if Magistrate Hathorne wants to talk to me about Goodwidow Blevins.

"Word is, they need people who can write pretty to record the doings at the examination, all legal and proper. If you turn up there tomorrow morning and offer your services, there could be coin in it for you."

"Why me, sir?"

"Simple. It's hard to find anyone willing to write up the notes, for fear he'll put down a mistake on the paper and some-body—either an accused person or the note writer—wakes up dead." He slices his index finger across his throat, which isn't strong encouragement for me to volunteer.

All the same, I'm curious about how the questioning will go for these accused witches, especially after what Sawtucket told us. Whatever fate awaits these women may soon come call-ing for more.

"If you're keen, I'll pass the word along," says Goodman Murdock. "You can go to Ingersoll's first thing tomorrow. And on Monday you can seek out Goodman Cawley."

Chapter 5
March 1

Patience

"For Heaven's sake, Abigail, hurry up! We don't want to miss a word of the examination." She might as well be a slug, so slowly is she moving.

"I've suffered grievously this day, sister. Have some patience," she growls from two paces behind me.

Last night we both suffered. I heard Abigail crying out beside me while we were meant to be asleep. Then she leaped out of bed, ran circles around our loft, and even raised the window as if to climb out. I had to drag her away from the window and pin her down on our bed until she stopped flailing. It was a mercy she didn't wake Dorothy, curled up at our feet. Even after Abigail dropped back to sleep, I lay awake wondering what was ailing her. Could it truly be witchcraft, the work of Sarah Good?

On the way to Ingersoll's inn, Abigail dodges a piebald sow that's broken loose of someone's yard. The goodwife is waving a switch and calling, "Sooie, sooie pig, come back here, you lout!"

"At any rate," Abigail mutters, "this examination can't be

such a spectacle if Mother is minding the fish stall instead of coming with us."

Oh, but she's wrong, which always delights me. It seems that the examination meant to be held at Ingersoll's has been moved to the meetinghouse on account of such a great crowd turning out to watch. By the time we reach the meetinghouse, most of Salem Village is crammed in, and more are peering through the window. We're slight, so we squeeze past burly yeomen to find a place to stand inside. I'm sure our toes will be trampled in the mob.

At the head of a large table by the pulpit sit John Hathorne and Jonathan Corwin, the magistrates who are to do the questioning. Reverend Parris is there too, armed with pen and ink to serve as one of the scribes. Near them stand the afflicted accusers: Ann Putnam, Abigail Williams, and the Elizabeths (Parris and Hubbard). Ann is twelve, Abigail eleven, and poor Betty Parris only nine. Elizabeth Hubbard is seventeen, barely two years my senior, but I've no acquaintance with her. As Dr. Griggs's niece she considers herself above our sort.

Abigail and I are pressed between two ripe-smelling old women—thank the good Lord it's nearly Saturday, bath night. I must stand on the tips of my toes to see over the motley crowd, which is how I spot the boy approaching the magistrates' table. He looks about my own age but carries himself with a man's dignity—though curiously, he doesn't remove his hat inside. Ah, a Quaker, I would guess. My breath catches. Quakers are well known to be dangerous heathens. They don't even baptize their young, so God alone knows what becomes of them when they leave this world.

I cannot hear what's being said at the magistrates' table. There seems to be a disagreement of some sort. Magistrate

Hathorne's brushy eyebrows are jumping as he pounds his hand on a stack of documents, sending them fluttering. His voice rises above the chaos. The only word I catch clear is "Sign!"

The boy shakes his head, shoulders squared. Who is he?

Thomas

Magistrate Hathorne's surprise flashes across his jowly face. "It is a requirement, young Stillbrooke. Else, how would we know you were recording these proceedings truly and fairly?

Moments before, I was yanked inside off the street by a servant who asked me, "You Thomas Stillbrooke what writes the King's English?"

"I am."

"Well and good. Come, we could use another scribe. One's inside, the good Reverend Parris, but t'other took sick in the belly." The servant dragged me in by the collar and pushed me up to the table, nearly into the magistrates' faces.

Now Magistrate Hathorne slides a document toward me. "You must take this oath, swearing that you will capture the proceedings as accurately as you can in the name of the king and queen, and then we can begin the inquiry."

We Friends do not swear oaths to earthly authorities, only to God. The lump in my throat is the size of a hummingbird. I've never had to stand up to a man as prominent as John Hathorne. My knees are knocking, the knobby bones clicking like ivory dice, but I keep my voice firm: "Sir, my word as a gentleman ought to be enough. Sir."

"A gentleman! You're all of fourteen, fifteen." He bangs his hand on the document between us. "And you cannot be a recorder of these events unless you sign the oath." He eyes my shabby clothes and leans forward to whisper, "The pay is three shillings."

I try not to leap out of my patched breeches. Three whole shillings—that's thirty-six pence. That would mean meat on our table once or twice, or a new frock and bonnet for Grace, who'll soon wear her clothing to rags with all her scrubbing and gardening for Goody Blevins. Three shillings, a fortune, and it is disappearing right before my eyes.

I back away and melt into the crowd, still poor.

Patience

The first of the three women to come before the magistrates is dark-skinned Tituba. I recognize her because she comes to our fish stall every week for flounder when we have it, cod when we don't. I've never spoken to her directly, though.

They're Indians from the island of Barbados, she and her husband John are, but they're not like the troublesome Wabanaki to the north and east. A year or two ago, the Wabanaki captured a maidservant barely older than myself—Mercy Short is her name. She was rescued by one of our men and now tells tales of the horrors she witnessed among her captors.

Reverend Parris always says that Indians, all Indians, are at war with God and have made unholy pacts with Satan. I've never quite understood why this is so. They're humans, aren't they? Like us?

But as soon as Tituba comes to stand before the magistrates, the four afflicted girls fall to the floor, writhing and moaning in agony. Two of them—Abigail Williams and

Betty Parris—live under the same roof as Tituba, so I suppose she would've found it easy enough to bewitch them all these weeks.

"That one's a witch for sure, as bad as Sarah Good," Abigail whispers to me, not taking her eyes off the suffering girls.

The gavel pounds the table, and Magistrate Hathorne's voice booms over the blustery crowd: "Why do you hurt these poor children?"

"I have done nothing," Tituba replies, eyes wide.

Abigail whispers, "She's lying, I can tell."

"Tell the truth," Magistrate Hathorne demands. "If not you, who is it that hurts those children?"

"The Devil, for all I know. I never see anything."

"What familiarity have you with the Devil?"

No answer as she looks from the magistrates to Reverend Parris, her master, who's eagerly recording the exchange.

The magistrates keep pressing her. "What is the Devil's appearance when he hurts the children?"

Tituba seems to be trying to decide just what to say, and we all hush in the short silence after her deep sigh. "He appears like a man. He commands me to serve him."

"I told you!" Abigail's breath is hot in my ear.

"In what appearance other than a man does the Devil appear to you?"

"Sometimes like a great black dog. Sometimes cats—one red, one black. They almost thrust me into the fire. Sometimes a hog."

A hog! The whole audience goes into a flurry at this news. There are even a few swine snorts.

Abigail and I share an astonished look. We know the Devil can unleash his evil in the guise of beasts, but a hog? Satan works in mysterious ways, I suppose. I myself have seen a little yellow canary lingering in the rafters of the meetinghouse from time to time, and I am certainly not a witch!

I remember Dorothy telling me about the snake that sucks blood from her finger. What am I to make of *that*?

"He said I must serve him six years," Tituba adds. "He commands me to hurt the girls, pinch and bite and twist them. But he said if I would not serve him, he would kill young Elizabeth Parris. I love Betty, I do. I must do as he says."

There it is—a confession.

Tituba hangs her head, and the magistrates look quite satisfied, as if their job is done and they look forward to going home for a little nap.

Thomas

What we're hearing from this woman Tituba is alarming to say the least. "The Devil tells me to tell nothing, tell no one," she says. "If I do, he would cut my head off."

I can't help but clutch my throat protectively.

But Magistrate Hathorne simply leans forward on his elbows and asks, "Where did you meet with the Devil?"

"In the pasture just beyond Reverend Parris's house, in the dark of night. But not I alone." Tituba speaks faster now. "Sarah Good and Sarah Osborne were there with me."

"And you went with these women, Sarah Osborne and Sarah Good, to meet with the Devil?"

"They are very strong. They pull me, make me go with them."

"How did you go? What did you ride upon?"

"I ride upon a stick or pole, and Good and Osborne behind me. I don't know how we go, for I saw no trees nor path, but we were presently there."

The questioning goes on and on. Reverend Parris records Tituba's words, as I would've been tasked with doing had I taken the oath. Tituba says that she has signed the Devil's book, where all his followers write their names or make their marks. Even more shocking, she claims there are not just three witches in Salem but *nine*.

That means there are other servants of the Devil among us, yet to be discovered. And if Tituba is telling the truth, then the witching and bewitching have gone far beyond pinches and twists.

But *is* this the truth, or is she spinning fantastical tales? I've gathered, from the whispers I've overheard, that she's enslaved to Reverend Parris. Whatever she says or does not say, he holds great power over her. So it stands to reason that she is choosing her words carefully, telling these men what they want to hear.

Finally, the magistrates formally accuse Tituba of covenanting with the Devil. The crowd is nearly silent now, so these words are clear: "Tituba is become a detestable witch against the peace of our sovereign lord and lady, the king and queen, their crown and dignity, and the laws in that case made and provided."

Tituba's hands are bound, and she's roughly led away.

And the constables bring in the next accused woman.

Chapter 6
March 1

Patience

"Sarah Good, what evil spirit have you familiarity with?" asks Magistrate Hathorne. The question is as pointed as a dagger. He doesn't even try to hide his anger.

"None! No evil spirit attaches itself to me!" She spits her words out in her usual disagreeable way, but then, who wouldn't be disagreeable upon being accused of witchcraft? Two men hold her at the elbows as if she might fly away. On a pole, perhaps!

The magistrates aren't a bit satisfied. Hathorne points to the clutch of afflicted girls and asks, "Why do you hurt these children?"

"I do not hurt them. I scorn it!"

"What creature do you use to hurt these children?"

"No creature do I use! I am falsely accused, this I swear!"

Magistrate Hathorne narrows his eyes to peer into Sarah Good's face. "Look about you. Do you not see now what you have done? Why do you not tell us the truth? Why do you torment these poor children?"

"I do *not* torment them, I tell you."

All around me, no one believes her.

The magistrates call witnesses. Elizabeth Hubbard speaks first. "Me, I saw Sarah Good torture the other three afflicted girls."

"Saw her bodily, with your own eyes?"

"Not Sarah Good herself—her apparition."

The others come forward, one at a time. "The apparition of Goody Good . . . a green light produced by the witch . . . a large white dog . . . some other beast I could not name . . . tortured me but not before enticing me to sign the Devil's book."

"They lie!" Sarah Good shrieks.

The crowd around me is shouting, and Magistrate Hathorne bangs on the table. "Order, order! Will another victim come forward to testify?"

Abigail steps toward the magistrates' table. My heart seizes. "You are?"

"Abigail Woodstock, sir," she answers timidly.

"Turn and look at Goody Sarah Good, child," Hathorne tells her. "Is she the one who has been hurting you?"

Abigail nods, but if she answers, her voice is so faint that no one can hear it.

"Recorder!" Magistrate Hathorne shouts above the noise of the crowd. "Note that the child has answered in the affirmative."

Suddenly Abigail is twitching violently, like the other afflicted girls. She drops to the floor and her pains send her flailing, her skirt flung up to her knees. I elbow my way through the mob to cover her petticoat and exposed skin by sitting on her.

Thomas

This newest girl writhing on the floor seems truly tormented—and is showing more limb than I ever expected to see before I marry. An older girl, about my age, throws herself upon the afflicted one, crying, "Abigail! Be calm! I have you." She looks familiar, but I can't place where I've seen her.

The other afflicted girls are beset with the same terrors, crying out about pinches and needle pricks. They do appear to be in great distress. But could they be cleverly pretending? To what end, though?

How glad I am not to be serving as a scribe. I couldn't have set down the details of these proceedings without sliding my own horror into the records.

Even with all these distractions, the magistrates relentlessly pummel Goodwife Sarah Good with accusations of covenanting with the Devil. I can see the woman is desperate to take the attention of the mob off herself.

"This I swear on my soul!" she hollers so all can hear. "It is Sarah Osborne who afflicts the girls. She's the one who signed the fiendish book out in Reverend Parris's pasture. Not I!"

But Magistrate Hathorne is not content with only one of the two Sarahs. "Once more, I ask you, Sarah Good, whom do you serve, God or Satan?"

"I serve only God, He who made Heaven and earth!" she shouts and spits, though fortunately the spittle falls short of the magistrates.

Her own husband, Goodman William Good, is called upon to testify. "As God is my witness," he declares, "I believe that my wife is either a witch now, or will be soon."

The crowd erupts with deafening voices. My stomach grinds. I cannot imagine Father testifying against Mother in a court of law. Though I also cannot imagine Mother being a witch.

My eyes are again drawn across the room to the girls who moan and twist on the floor, and my gaze drifts to the older girl straddling one of them, holding her down in her torment. Ah, now I know where I've seen the older girl—in the market square. She's the fishmonger's daughter. Patience, I've heard her called. Patience Woodstock.

"Have you witnessed any evil deeds she's performed?" Hathorne asks William Good.

"No, sir, I have not, not with me own eyes. But these same eyes have seen the Devil's mark just below her shoulder, looking like a teat what the Devil's beast could suckle." Goodman Good squares his shoulders proudly, thumbs tucked under his coat collar. "I may say with tears that she is an enemy to all good."

Patience

I manage to lift my sister to her feet and half carry, half drag her off to one side of the room, away from the other afflicted girls. Meanwhile, Sarah Osborne is brought in and the questioning shifts to her. While the magistrates demand to know why Goody Osborne has been absent from Lord's Day meetings for so long—and dismiss her protests that she's been too ill to attend—Abigail slowly relaxes and stands upright, though she keeps her hands splayed in front of her like a knight's shield against anything Goody Good might do to her.

I'm still stewing over Goody Good's interrogation. All the evidence against her comes from people who didn't actually see *her* but saw her specter or the beasts called her familiars, creature-servants of the Devil merely representing her. And her accusers are her faithless husband, another confessed witch, and a handful of girls who may be addled by their suffering. How can we be certain they're not mistaken about whom those specters and familiars represent?

Across the room, I notice the boy who stood so tall before the magistrates earlier. He's not trembling, as I'm told Quakers do when their God speaks to them directly—as if God would ever do such a thing! Instead, he's still and planted as an elm, while everyone else is clamoring and shrieking and tearing about the room. His somber gaze snags on mine. I immediately lower my eyes and tuck my petticoats around my heels.

Magistrate Hathorne brusquely declares that all three of the accused women will be held in chains until a proper court can be convened to try them for their crimes. Sarah Osborne and Tituba will be taken to Salem Town's jail, while Sarah Good will be sent a half-day's journey to the jail in Boston.

"They lie, all of them!" Sarah Good screams as two gruff yeomen jerk her up so her feet kick air. They haul her away while she curses the magistrates with language such as I've never heard except from sailors on the harbor docks.

Thomas

The magistrates might as well convict Sarah Good here and now—why wait for a trial? Just sentence her to hang, because everyone in the room is convinced she is a witch. Perhaps they would be less inclined to condemn her if she were not so surly and spiteful in her responses. I know what Grace would say:

Apparently Goodwife Good's mother did not teach her that honey catches flies sooner than vinegar.

It's by mercy alone that Grace isn't here to witness this day's horrors.

We Friends believe that we are born with pure souls and that evil befalls us when we are separated from God through ignorance and wicked deeds—of which there are plenty, as my father taught me. But our Puritan neighbors work all through their lives to overcome the evil they're born with. So, if a person looks and speaks and acts evil, as the pipe-smoking Sarah Good does, cursing and spitting and mocking the magistrates—well then, she must *be* evil and a willing host to the Devil.

But the Devil is known to be a great deceiver. Can he not make the guilty look innocent and the innocent seem guilty? So it troubles me that Sarah Good and Sarah Osborne may be condemned without any firm proof of wrongdoing. And now that Tituba has said there are *more* witches, the investigations will surely continue. Others may come under suspicion with just as little evidence.

A memory comes to me from far back in my childhood. One afternoon, Father plucked a red apple from the tree behind our house and tossed it to me. It landed with a satisfying thud in my hand. I'd eaten a fair number of apples in my five years and knew their merits well. This one's deep color and sweet fragrance begged me to sink my teeth into it. But Father said, "Thomas, I ask thee not to taste this apple."

"Why?" I cried, taunted by the perfect object, cool and heavy in my palm.

"Thee must think first about each deed, my son. What does it mean? What is thy responsibility?"

I felt certain I had *no* responsibility for a mere piece of fruit that grew plentifully in our garden. Anger at my father surged through me, and I threw the apple to the ground, watching it smash. At that spiteful moment, I condemned it to become food for the worms of the earth.

Only later did I understand what my father meant that day, a decade past now: that all our deeds have consequences.

Do the people of Salem understand that simple truth?

Chapter 7
Early March

Thomas

We have drifted into an arrangement with the mistress of our new home, who demands that we call her Pru.

"Oh, Goodwidow Blevins, that would be highly disrespectful," Grace protests.

The old woman glares at us with rheumy eyes. "Ach, why should I bandy about the name of that worthless miscreant Obadiah Blevins? Pru, that's my name. Short and to the point."

Grace cooks and washes and looks after the woman's needs, walking her to the privy out back at all hours of the day and night, and Pru never utters a word of thanks. But Grace is more generous than I am. "Then we shall call you *Goody* Pru," she announces, and there's no further discussion.

On First Day—what our neighbors call the Lord's Day— Grace and I each lock an arm through Pru's and we walk, as slow as snails, to the Puritan meetinghouse. By the time we get there, dreary psalms, recited by rote, are already pouring out the open windows. We settle Goody Pru into the back row, with at least two empty seats on either side of her, and she laments, "I suppose you'll be going on to that Godforsaken

Quaker meetinghouse. Quakers are servants of the Devil, don't you know?"

It seems to me that we are servants of Goody Pru, but there's no point in arguing with her. Our Puritan neighbors do not like Friends—or Baptists or Catholics, for that matter. We are none of us pious enough to meet their standards.

On we trudge to the Friends' meetinghouse, which is suitably plain and without a showy steeple like the Puritan meetinghouse has. Inside, only a handful of families are gathered, men on one side, women on the other. The meeting throbs with silence, broken only by an occasional cough or sneeze or sucking of teeth, or by the chattering of a flock of geese outside.

As we wait for God to shed His light upon us, my soul remains dark. We have lost so much and gained so little by coming across the sea.

Grace rests her head on my shoulder and drifts off. My arm goes numb from the weight of her, but at least one side of my body is warm—for it's as dark and cold as a tomb in the meetinghouse.

A Friend behind us has appointed himself the official pincher for those who fall to dozing. "No snoring!" he hisses, poking Grace. I've felt the well-intentioned nipping of my own skin a few times as well. Disapproving looks remind me that my sister should not even be sitting with me. Next week I shall have to send her to the women's section where she has no mother to comfort her, while I sit alone among the men.

My mind refuses to stay quiet. It races through the odd events that have turned Salem topsy-turvy: girls twinged and pricked with pins, choked, led to fire. Three women jailed for witchcraft, and more suspected of it. Is there justice in all this bedlam?

The pinching Friend must sense that I'm distracted from seeking my own Inner Light. He prods my shoulder, and I snap to attention. So, I am not a good shipbuilder, not yet tested as a cordwainer, and here I am, not a good member of the Society of Friends. What *am* I good for?

Come next week, when Goodman Cawley returns from his business in Boston, I shall try to find out.

Patience

"The Lord does terrible things amongst us," Reverend Parris says, "by lengthening the chain of the roaring lion, so that the Devil is come down in great wrath."

It's not clear to me how a lion gets mixed up in this matter, so my attention drifts. I'm shivering in this drafty meeting-house, but at least I'm not seized by fits like the bewitched girls. They've fared no better since their tormentors were jailed. Now they say they're afflicted by other witches among us. Word has it that, as Tituba swore, swarms of witches gather in Reverend Parris's pasture in the dark of night. They eat and drink red bread and blood and sign their names in a forbidden book. This is how they pledge their lives to the Devil, he with the black hat (some say it's white) and black cloak (some say it's red), hungry to ensnare their immortal souls.

Repentance, that's what I must be about, especially since I'll soon turn fifteen, when I must profess my conversion in front of the whole congregation, so I can elevate from a Half Covenant with God to a Full Covenant. The only hope for my soul is to repent of my many sins, whatever they may be.

The wooden pew is straight and stiff such that I can't help

but sit upright, all the better to concentrate on the stirring sermon. But Reverend Parris's words float around me like smoke. "Fellow saints, mark me well . . ."

Abigail says she's been dragged from our house at midnight on her belly like a snake. In the mornings she looks ragged, her eyes rimmed in red, her hair a wild nest, and her belly raw.

We've always shared a bed, my sister and I, and Abigail has grudgingly welcomed Dorothy to warm our feet with her small body. Well, Dorothy sleeps like a rock sunk in water, but since I am a very light sleeper I would know if Abigail were dragged away. In fact, if she had been, I would have followed.

Now, though, Abigail points at fluttering wings in the rafters above us. Swallows often fly in through the windows Reverend Parris leaves open, else our meetinghouse would be nearly as dark as a jail cell. But it's not a swallow that's taken refuge here. It's that yellow canary I've seen before. Could it be a witch's familiar?

I no longer know what to think.

Chapter 8
Early March

Thomas

The sweet scent of tanned leather draws me into the cordwainer's shop. Embers from a smothered fire shoot jeweled sparks into the small room that's crowded with all the tools of the trade. There is no one in sight—not Goodman Cawley, nor any customer—so I'm free to look around at the wooden forms made into the shapes of shoes, at the soft hide cloths blackened with polish. I slide into the worn curve of the shoemaker's bench. The mallets and pliers are fitted to my hand. Unlike at the shipyard, where everything is massive, here things are scaled to human needs: feet, hands.

I'm hit by a blast of late-winter chill as the door flies open. A giant of a man fills the threshold. Like me, he wears knee breeches and a rumpled linen shirt, though no topcoat as would befit a Friend. Instead, he has a leather cape around his shoulders and a leather apron over the front of his breeches. His voice booms: "Who are you, boy?"

"Thomas Stillbrooke, sir."

"Looks of you, doubt you come to buy shoes. Not that anyone does."

"No, sir, I do not come to buy shoes. I come to make them." I'm astonished at my own boldness, but what other choice do I have? I cannot afford to fail again if we're to have bread and ale on Goody Pru's table for the three of us.

Goodman Cawley hitches up his apron, which sags from the stiffened weight of the leather. "No money in it," he says gruffly. "These local bumpkins think they do better importing their boots from London. Find some other trade. I'm busy."

I can't guess what he'd be busy doing if he has no customers, but he picks up a dried-out boot and massages oil into it. Life, breath, color return to the stiff leather, and the scent deepens.

"You still here, boy?"

"I am, sir, yes."

"Nervy fellow, aren't you?"

There's no good answer to that. I'm at this man's mercy. My mind wanders to the ragged, mute man in London who used to come up and down our lane with a mop and bucket that he'd push into each house that answered his knock. Mother, bless her soul, would let him in to run his mop around our spotless floor for a penny and a mug of cold cider.

"Goodman Cawley, I know how we could stir up business."

"We?"

"Yes, sir, we."

While the shoemaker polishes the old boot, I reach for one of the shoe forms hanging from a nail on the wall—smooth wood carved in the shape of a human foot, wide at the heel, narrow at the toe. "Sir, I could take this around to houses all over Salem and promise people that we could have new shoes for them quicker than waiting for a tired ship from England, and cheaper by half."

"Ha!" He's furiously oiling the boot now, because I've

gotten under his skin. "Ever made a shoe? Cut a tough piece of leather? Pounded hobnails?"

"No, sir, but I'm a quick learner. Just ask Goodman Murdock the shipwright." *Pray he doesn't!*

He studies me for a good long minute. "Mark my words, you won't nab a single pitiful order."

"Then you won't pay me." *I still have two pence jiggling in my pocket.*

"Pay you? You expect me to pay you, boy? With what? I'm half-starving myself."

"Soon we'll have more business than you can manage. In the mornings I'll get the promises, and in the afternoons I'll come here and help you make the shoes to fit each man, woman, and child in Salem."

No answer from the shoemaker, but I've heard that patience is a virtue. I stand spine-straight, gaze fixed on him as if I can move his heart by the rays of my eyes. The wooden shoe form grows warm in my palm.

He chews on the inside of his mouth as if it were shoe leather, or better yet, a hunk of mutton. "If perchance you got an order, you'd have to write it down in my ledger." He flashes a leather-bound book under my eyes, open to blank pages. Setting pen and ink on the worktable before me, he asks, "Can you write pretty, boy?"

Does he mean pretty penmanship or pretty words? I'd best cover both, so I write in the book, *The wheel is come full circle: I am here.*

Goodman Cawley wrinkles his brow. "Looks right pretty, I'll say that much."

"It's from Shakespeare, sir." Though I've never seen one of his plays performed, I've read the printed texts of his works.

"And what use is that to me, boy? What wheel do you write of?"

"I only mean I am here to be of service to you, if you'll allow it."

"Can't take you on as an apprentice," he grumbles.

"I'll just come by each day and work for pennies until you can."

Goodman Cawley grunts, sounding like one of the wild boars I've seen in the forest nearby. I take his grunt to mean we are partners for now. I'll set about my task immediately. Which house shall I call upon first?

I pick up the wooden form again and reach for another, a size that I'd guess would fit Grace or, hmm, perhaps a girl two or three years older. Miss Patience Woodstock, the elder of the fishmonger's daughters, comes to mind.

Patience

My hands are dusty with flour when I answer the sharp knock at the door. To my surprise, there stands the Quaker boy I saw at the witches' examination. He seems equally startled to see me as I clap my hands together to release a cloud of gray flour dust.

He clears his throat and affects a deep voice that I suspect isn't yet his. "I am Thomas Stillbrooke, the shoemaker's apprentice." Stepping straight into the house, he proudly thrusts something toward me as if it were a posy or a quail ready for the cookpot, but no, it's a rounded wooden block. What on earth?

"And what brings you to my door, Thomas Stillbrooke, the shoemaker's apprentice? I already have a fine pair of shoes."

I angle my foot toward him, and too late I remember the eye-sized hole at my toe.

"We can mend that, Miss Patience, for a most reasonable price."

"Shall I go about town with one shoe?" Quickly I slip my foot back under my skirt. "And how do you know my name?"

He flushes, and I notice the faint freckles that dot his cheeks. He has not taken his hat off, despite having the gall to enter the house uninvited. "Walking through the market square, I've heard your mother call you and your sister, Miss Abigail."

"Ah, well, Heaven itself knows that my mother has a mighty voice. It could call birds out of the sky."

"I was also at the examination of Goodwife Sarah Good. I believe I saw you sitting on your sister's limbs," he says, a half smile expanding his freckles. He sounds almost as if he means to tease me. "I hope she'll recover now that the woman that she's accused is locked up."

At this moment Abigail is in the loft with Dorothy and her hornbook, teaching the child her letters. "Say after me: *ah, ah, beh, beh, cee dee eee*." What a silly poem. I've always struggled with those stupefying sounds, myself. Next I suppose Abigail will have the child learning to write, though I can't imagine that Dorothy will ever need such knowledge. We have scribes among us to do that troublesome chore—men who could never bake a loaf of rye or Indian corn if their very lives hinged on it.

At least Abigail isn't thrashing about in torment just now. In fact, she and Dorothy poke their heads out from the loft to see who's standing in our hearth room.

I'm still bristling at Thomas Stillbrooke's words. "Who are you to offer us well-wishes?" This boy unsettles me. We faithful saints suspect Quakers of Devil worship—or worse, being one and the same with the Devil. This boy has no right to pity us, God's chosen children.

"I meant to give no offense," Thomas says.

"Well, you're certainly bold for a Quaker." Generally they keep to themselves, and with good cause. Four of his kind were hanged in Boston a few years ago. The luckier ones were merely whipped and jailed. Father says some had holes bored into their tongues to keep them from spouting their heresy. Oh, mercy, the whole idea makes me shiver with dread.

At the very moment this ghastly image runs through my head, Dorothy drops her hornbook over the edge of the loft. It misses Thomas's head by a whisper of an inch.

He snaps up the wooden tablet and stretches to hand it back to Dorothy. "I trust you didn't mean to flatten my head with this."

"Oh, no, sir," Dorothy cries. "It just slipped out of my hands."

"I had slippery hands at your age too, Miss . . . ?"

"Dorothy," she says. "Dorothy Good."

"Ah." His face softens. He must recognize the name, new to Salem though he is. The names of witches travel fast. "I hope you make good progress with your lessons, Miss Dorothy. Just mind that you keep a firm hold on that hornbook."

She giggles, and I smile in spite of myself at his gently playful tone.

Abigail looks from Thomas to Dorothy to me and back to Thomas. Her brow furrows deeply, and I think of Mother's warning that our faces will freeze that way if we're not careful.

My sister's disapproving gaze ought to put me on my guard. The boy should go at once. And yet I find myself asking him another question to delay his leaving. "Do you live in Salem Village?"

"Aye, Miss Patience. My sister Grace and I are staying with Goodwidow Prudence Blevins."

At this, Abigail scrambles down the ladder, her skirt fluttering behind her. "Goodwidow Blevins? Aren't you afraid for your life? She's one of them, you know."

"Them?" Thomas asks.

"Them! The witches, who else? No different from"—she points up to the loft—"her mother." She whispers to spare Dorothy the hurt.

We've never even spoken to old Goodwidow Blevins—or to be fair, she's never spoken to us. I've heard some call her a witch, but I always took that for mere grumbling. I've not heard of her actually bewitching anyone.

Thomas frowns. "Have you evidence of her evil deeds, Miss Abigail?"

"I most certainly do. She came to my bed and woke me two nights past. Twisted my arm behind my back until I was sure it would hang like a loose bone inside my skin."

Oh, dear. It's preposterous! I would have heard something, seen something. I must get Thomas out of our house before he concludes that our whole family is mad.

"Thomas, you must go. It is not proper for you to be here with us, and no chaperone in sight."

"Yes, but will you consider Goodman Cawley's shop for a new pair of shoes? Or we could mend the shoe you showed me."

I feel my face redden at the thought of removing my shoe in this boy's presence. "I am managing quite well with my tiny toe hole, thank you." I flap a hand to usher him out. Once he's beyond our threshold, I watch him strut jauntily up the lane as if he hasn't a care on his heart.

He should have more caution.

Chapter 9
Mid-March

Thomas

Come evening, I'm still turning the strange meeting with the Woodstocks over in my mind. At the forefront, of course, are Abigail Woodstock's accusations against Goody Pru. What an odd girl, that one. Her eyes are flat, and she's never still for a moment. Perhaps before she was bewitched, she was more like the other daughter, the feisty Miss Patience.

And then there's Sarah Good's daughter, Dorothy. It seems that the Woodstocks have taken her in. She has such a lost look about her. The poor child has a witch bound for Gallows Hill for a mother and a betrayer for a father.

There are worse fates than being orphans, as Grace and I are.

Grace stirs a pot of hasty pudding with one hand, blowing to cool a spoonful she holds in the other. Goody Pru stands behind her on feet so swollen that they hang over her shoes like bread dough. I look at the holes in the cracked leather of her shoes, and suddenly it occurs to me that I've somehow lost one of the wooden shoe forms that I brought around town with me earlier.

Somehow? I know exactly how. I left it at the fishmonger's house. I'm no better as a cordwainer than I was as a shipbuilder.

I'm a passable fish-gutter, though. Goodwife Woodstock let me have a mackerel for a penny because the flabby fish was left at the end of the day and no doubt spoiled. We'll all be poisoned by morning, but at least we'll die with our bellies full for a change. My fingers smell of dead fish, and I wonder how the fishmonger and her daughters ever get the stink off their hands.

I smelled no whiff of fish about Miss Patience earlier today. I can still picture her as I saw her this afternoon. Wisps of her brown hair hang below her bonnet, as shiny as a kitten's back, and her eyes are the green of—

Grace looks up from the stir-pot of cornmeal mush. "Brother, thee is blushing!"

Goody Pru grumbles, "Has the fever, no doubt. Work of the Devil. What have you done, boy, to bring on the wrath of God?" Our Pru is always full of good cheer.

"I do nothing but work for our keep," I say. "Which is how I've been bringing in a penny or two each day."

"Those pennies that keep us away from the wolf's mouth," Grace adds. "How else could we have had succotash and warm ale to wash it down at our noonday meal?" No mention of tonight's fish, but I can scarcely blame her for that.

Pru waddles over to slap a bony palm over my brow. "He isn't burning up, but you never can tell. If he's not dead by the Lord's Day, he'll probably live to spring."

Unless the mackerel does us in.

Yes, that's it, spring. Eyes the green of new spring buds, has Miss Patience. I shall have to go back to reclaim Goodman Cawley's shoe form.

Later, when Goody Pru is deep in sleep, I whisper to Grace what Abigail Woodstock told me about Pru.

Grace scowls. "I don't believe it. Surely she's done no real harm to anybody."

"I would've thought not, but the Woodstock girl was so sure."

Grace scowls and cants her head toward Pru. "Then we must ask her."

The woman can still hear. Her eyes snap open. "Ask me what?"

"The best place in the forest to find gingerwort," Grace says quickly.

Snorting, Goody Pru says, "Ach, don't put your mind to herbs and teas. They're mine."

Grace settles the woman back under her comforter. "Sleep, Goody Pru. My brother and I will be right outside."

"Shut the door behind you. It's bone cold," she snaps and drops into sleep again with her mouth hanging open and her tongue out as if to catch flies.

Outside, my teeth chatter as ice pinpricks my cheeks.

Grace says, "Thee must put this suspicion of thine to rest— or at least have the decency to let Goody Pru speak for herself instead of nursing doubts in secret."

What if she casts us out? I can't bring myself to ponder what might happen to us then. "I'll brave it tomorrow, first thing," I promise. "I'll come right out and ask her if the rumors are true about her being a witch."

Grace is stomping her feet to keep the blood flowing. "I should be the one to ask her."

"Leave it to me. I'm more diplomatic."

"Pah, what's diplomacy compared to truthfulness?"

Justly peeved, I mutter, "I am the head of this family."

"And I am the foot that keeps marching ahead. Tomorrow, then. Don't wait another day, brother, not one more day."

Patience

Day by day, the afflicted girls add names to their list of bewitchers. Talk of the gallows lingers like thick fog in the air. It is Father's favorite subject. He sits at our table while Mother and Abigail and I stand, our trenchers lifted to our chins, and Dorothy plays with wooden spoons in the corner. I dance my feet as usual, until I kick something across the room.

"What is that?" Mother asks as the wooden object clatters against the wall.

The wooden block that Thomas Stillbrooke left in my haste to shoo him out the door!

Abigail eyes it curiously. "It's a doll, just without hair and clothing, not even fit for Dorothy over there. Eyes and lips need to be carved out of it." She turns it round and round. "No, it's a giant ancient potato, petrified into wood. What do you think, Patience?"

I only shrug. If I tell Mother and Father that Thomas Stillbrooke was in this very room, alone with us girls, they'll be furious!

Mother picks it up with her apron, as if it were a dead rat, and places it on the table. "I've never seen the likes of this. Have you, husband?"

Father pushes it with his spoon, spitting out a fish bone to join the small hill of them on his plate. "A witch's instrument if ever I did see one."

Abigail says, "Do you think the witch Goody Blevins sent it to us by . . ." She pauses here and throws a dark look my way. ". . . by her messenger?"

My heart is in my throat. She's a breath away from telling our parents about Thomas Stillbrooke.

"What's this talk of Goody Blevins?" asks Mother. "We'd barely recognize the woman if she passed us in the lane."

"Never mind, wife," says Father, twisting round on the bench to reach behind him. He has a mighty reach, as befits a fisherman. "I know where this evil thing comes from," he says, prodding Dorothy with his spoon, but he still won't speak to her directly. "The waif brought this Devil's token into our home."

Dorothy fairly shouts, "I didn't!" And Abigail clamps her hand over Dorothy's mouth.

The blood rises in Father's face and his cheeks puff out. "I heard her. Tell the vixen that I will abide no lying in my house."

Mother rushes to calm the storm: "Whatever it is, it must have been blown into the house in the heavy wind this morning, husband. Now, finish your soup before the fat clumps on it."

"It didn't blow in," Dorothy whispers, and I pinch her elbow to hush her, but Father doesn't hear her over his sucking of the flesh off the fish's spine.

Thomas

Spring hangs back in this beastly cold, damp country where sap freezes on logs in the hearth. Still, I'm strolling home the long way after a day with Goodman Cawley. The good thing about him, for all his melancholy, is that he does not talk about the witchcraft troubles. Everyone else in Salem can talk of nothing else.

I'm in no hurry to confront Goody Pru, so I wander into Salem Town and pause when I spot that beggar who directed us the day we arrived in the Bay Colony. Wrapped in his tattered topcoat, he's still perched on his boulder as if he's never left it all these weeks. A short wooden stem sticks out of his mouth, lodged in the wide space between two jagged front teeth.

"Sawtucket, is it?"

"At yer service." He doffs his hat as he did the day we disembarked. "Balmy day, wouldja say, lad?"

"Balmy, not yet. But at least I can walk without pelting snow pushing me into the wind howling at my back."

"Ye're a poet, sayin' troofs so elegant." I suppose he means *truths*. "Ye find the shipwright?"

"So, you remember us."

"Sweet young lassy with ye, how could I forget?" His hand opens one finger at a time until his palm is flat, poised to welcome a coin. Seeing that I don't reach into my pocket, he claps his hands together as if he's patting biscuit dough. "Lodgin' over in the Village with the widow Blevins, best of me recollection. She done anythin' peculiar?"

"Everything she does is peculiar."

He cackles and sucks on that stem in his mouth as if it produces sweet juice. "Didn't I warn ye?"

＊

After supper, Grace and I are putting the trenchers up on the shelf above the hearth and whispering so Goody Pru won't hear us from her bed across the room. Her swollen feet are elevated on wooden blocks I've borrowed from Goodman Cawley's shop.

Pru doesn't see well, but those ears! "You two urchins, what're you going on about? Speak up or I'll throw my shoe at you." Her hand pats around on the floor. "Grace, reach me my shoe."

Grace says sweetly, "I'm afraid you've forgotten your manners, Goody."

"My shoe. Please. If it please you. By your leave, you churlish harpy," she snarls.

"Much better," says Grace, nodding to me that it's the right time. I've done a splendid job of putting it off. Avoidance is a special talent of mine.

We pull the bench over to her bed. I'm pondering how to start when Grace blurts out, "Salem people say you are a witch."

"Do they now?" The old woman's voice is cold and hard.

I pat Grace's knee to keep her quiet. "There are rumors, Goody."

Pru turns toward the wall, yanking her threadbare blanket with her and kicking the wooden blocks that support her swollen feet. Every movement looks painful.

Gently, I touch her shoulder. "Deny it, Goody Pru, and we will believe you."

She lets out a groan. "See me? I am old and worn out, no stronger than this faded rag of a blanket. How could I go about bewitching people, I ask you?"

Grace's glance says *I told thee, brother.*

Twisting her head to look at us, Goody Pru adds, "Have I left the house even once, except to go to meeting on the Lord's Day and out back to do my business? And even then Grace is with me through every drop."

Which is more than I needed to know. "We've heard certain people say they see you out and about. The fishmonger's daughter, Miss Abigail—she says you came to her bedside two nights ago and twisted her arm until she thought it would break loose."

"Hmm." Goody Blevins reaches a shaky hand out to mine and squeezes. There is no more pressure in those bony fingers than in a breeze.

"So, you are *not* a witch?" Grace presses, to prove her point.

"Ah, that is the bewitching question," she says, cackling through the missing teeth, and with that, her eyes close like two peepholes slammed in our faces.

Chapter 10
Mid-March

Patience

Spiders are such untidy creatures, but so clever. I'm standing in front of our house, sweeping cobwebs from the eaves, when I sense someone behind me.

"Miss Patience?"

Thomas, the shoemaker's apprentice! My heart takes a small leap, and I sweep furiously until the cobwebs and any lingering dead spiders are smashed to a paste.

"I left something at your house that belongs to my master, Goodman Cawley."

"Ah," I say with my back to him, hiding my smile. "The petrified potato."

"Potato? No, I mean the wooden shoe form that we use to mimic a foot."

"Is that what it is? Wait here." I rush inside, glad that Mother has dragged Abigail to the market, so only Dorothy is here to see me fetch Thomas's curious object. When I step back outside and pass it to him, pleased at the smile spreading across his freckled face, I tell him, "If you ask me, it does not look at all like a foot. Where are the toes?"

Thomas laughs as he weighs the wooden block in his long, thin hand. "I suppose the toes are left to our imagination."

"My father thought this was a witch's relic that Dorothy Good smuggled into our Christian home. Lucky for all of us that he didn't suspect it was a Quaker token."

Thomas asks with a laugh, "What tokens do you think we wield?"

"How should I know? You're the first Quaker I've ever been near enough to speak to. For all I know this could be a statue of one of your saints, without toes *and* without a head."

"We keep no statues, and our saints are not made of wood. They're flesh and bone—mere mortals who answer God's call."

"Oh. We are called saints too!" Finally, something we have in common. "So, this wooden block, it is not a kneeler, such as the Catholics use?"

"We neither kneel nor bow, and unlike you, we have no ministers."

"Oh, mercy! Are you even Christians?"

"We are, though each of us finds his own path to God and to life in the world beyond."

But this is heresy! God decides our fate from the moment we are born! "You sound even stranger than the Catholics."

"We are nothing like Catholics. For one thing, they celebrate so-called holy days, like Christmas. Your people and mine do not. We Friends believe that every day is holy."

I try to seem composed, knowledgeable. "Well, at any rate, Christmas is a pagan holiday. There's not one word about it in the Bible. Do you read the same Bible we do?"

"Of course. There is but one."

At that moment Dorothy dashes out of the house, yelling, "They're coming! The bad men are coming!"

I glance about and see no one in the lane, only the customary roaming pigs and chickens and geese out for a stroll on this unusually warm March day.

Barely a moment has passed, me clutching the broom as if it were a weapon, when Goodman Putnam and Goodman Herrick come around the back of our neighbor's house.

How is it possible that Dorothy saw the men before they appeared? From the loft window, up high? The child has such rare sensitivities. Perhaps that comes from being the daughter of a witch.

I scurry into the house with Dorothy, and Thomas boldly follows as if he belongs in our humble home. Dorothy scampers up the ladder to the loft. I'm embarrassed to be standing alone with this boy again. We stare at one another in stunned silence as the two constables step to my open door.

"Where is the head of this house?" Goodman Putnam asks gruffly.

"Out on the water," I say, hoping I sound grown. "You can speak with me."

Goodman Herrick unfurls a formal document. "We've come for the child Dorcas Good. This is a warrant for her arrest."

He clearly means Dorothy. I gasp and clap a hand to my heart. "Her arrest! On what charge?"

"Witchcraft, same as her mother. Ann Putnam and Mary Walcott have both accused her."

Mary Walcott is a niece of Goodwife Sibley, who directed Tituba and John to make that witch-cake and feed it to the dog. I can't imagine what harm Dorothy could've brought to these girls. Is she to be put through an examination as her mother was, when she's not yet five years?

Thomas must be thinking along the same path. He says, "But she's just a child."

"Who are you?" Goodman Herrick barks as he stows the warrant back in his pouch and slides a thick rope through his fingers. A rope meant to tie up poor Dorothy. No!

"Thomas Stillbrooke, sir."

"Stillbrooke? Goodman Putnam, do we know a Stillbrooke family?"

"Newcomers. Quakers. The *enlightened ones,*" his companion says with a sneer.

I sneak a look at Thomas out of the corner of my eye. The boy is so comely and polite and learned, and infuriating, and is indeed a Quaker, with all their strange ways. Yet in other ways, he does not seem so different from us.

"Where's the witch child?" Goodman Herrick demands.

God forgive me, I have a mind to lie, for Dorothy has been entrusted to my care. But lying is a mortal sin. I cannot.

I resolve to take refuge in silence. If I say nothing, that is not a lie.

But Thomas says, "She's gone to the well with a bucket, sir."

Thomas

Why did I say the child had gone to fetch water, when I knew it wasn't true? When did I become a person who'd lie so freely?

But these men who've come for Dorothy, they look fierce and dangerous, with that ominous rope nearly thick enough to anchor one of Goodman Murdock's ships.

To be sure, though, there's something peculiar about this child—an otherworldly quality about her. She *seemed* to see these two men coming before they'd turned the corner. Could one so young possibly be a witch?

It's difficult to say whether I lied to protect the child or to impress Miss Patience, who's so distressed over the men's errand. She gazes at me wide-eyed now—probably fearing for my immortal soul.

One of the men sets off toward the well to look for Dorothy. The other man waits in front of the fishmonger's house, pacing and snapping the rope against the fence pickets.

Miss Patience steps closer to me inside the dark house and whispers, "I will not give Dorothy to them. Never."

Her eyes are so fierce that despite all reason, I believe her—and am ready to help her however I can.

Patience

"Is there a way out the back?" Thomas whispers.

"Only a small window."

"We could stuff the child out through there."

I scurry up the ladder to the loft.

Dorothy crouches in the corner. "Patience?"

"Hush, little one," I whisper. "You must be very quiet. Can you do that?"

"I can," she whispers back, her voice no louder than a feather falling.

"Good. Stay still now and let me carry you." I wrap her in my patchwork blanket, pick her up, and ease my way back down the ladder. Thomas holds it steady for me.

With Thomas at my heels, I rush to the back window, unlatch it, and push it open. "Now," I tell the trembling child, "you must hasten out the window as quiet as a beetle and run as far and as fast as you can."

"Where's Mama?"

"Just run, Dorothy, do you understand me?"

I wedge her through the window and hear her land with a thud on the hard winter ground. The blanket goes flying, and that crow that seems always to perch outside our window swoops down and grabs the edge of the cloth in his beak.

Dorothy leaps to her feet, but as soon as she begins to run I hear a gruff voice.

"The well, indeed!" Goodman Putnam shouts. "Come quick, Joseph, I have the fish in my net!"

I race outside, hoping to distract the men. But Goodman Putnam has already caught Dorothy and now holds her in his grasp, while Goodman Herrick approaches with the rope.

"Bind her up!" Goodman Putnam orders. "She's thrashing like a tiger. Just like her demon mother. I can't hold her much longer."

"Where are you taking her?" I shout, but I'm ignored. I do not tolerate being ignored. "I demand to know where you're taking the child!"

"If you must know," says Goodman Herrick as he winds the rope around her tiny wrists, "we'll toss her in the Ipswich jail. She can rot there till the Second Coming, for all I care."

I'm tempted to rake my fingernails down the man's leathery neck, to pull Dorothy to safety, but he already has her hands bound with the rope. She hangs like a cape from Goodman Putnam's back, kicking mightily until Goodman Herrick ropes her ankles as well.

I'll be no match for these men on my own. "Thomas Stillbrooke, for Heaven's sake, help me!" I shout.

The shoemaker's apprentice seems stupefied, frozen in place.

The men set off down the road, with Dorothy yelling like a banshee. The black crow stares down at us. The ribbons of my bonnet flutter in the breeze. I'm suddenly chilled to the bone, and I clasp my arms modestly around myself.

I look up to Thomas's stricken face. "Clear as sunrise, those horrid men were harming an innocent child!" Dorothy *is* innocent, isn't she? Of course she is. "And you did nothing, nothing at all!"

"It is our way, in the Society of Friends," Thomas tells me. "Do not lift a hand to do violence to another."

"You are a prisoner of your faith," I say hotly. "And as much use to your neighbors as that crow there."

"Raven, not crow," Thomas says. "You can tell by its wedged tail feathers." The bird spreads its tail feathers as if it understands our words.

Tears blur my eyes. "How do you come to be such an authority on black birds?"

"I know ravens. They guard the Tower of London." He grimaces. "I wish I were in London now."

"I was born here in Salem. I know nothing of your London," I reply crossly. I am quite sure I despise Thomas Stillbrooke. "You must leave at once. It is highly improper for you to be here. If Mother finds you, she'll see that the minister hears of it and then I'll be put to shame for my sinfulness."

Quietly, Thomas echoes my words: "You are a prisoner of your faith."

"Go!"

He does, and immediately I wish he hadn't.

Chapter 11
Late March

Thomas

It's true, what I told Miss Patience: our way is to do no harm to any other human being. But that is only partly why I stood by as those men took Dorothy. What flashed through my mind at that moment was a miserable memory from January.

Mother was heavy with child. A few weeks before we Stillbrookes were to leave for the Massachusetts Bay Colony, Mother suddenly collapsed to the floor, doubled over in a puddle of pinkish water, her face the color of limestone. "Thomas! Run for Maudey the midwife. Above the butcher's. Grace will stay here and attend to me until Maudey comes."

Grace turned as white as Mother, her arms wrapped round her own middle. I was almost out the door when Mother said, "Fetch thy father as well, Thomas. Tell him . . ." She clutched her belly as a wave of pain tore through her. "Tell him it's dire."

The butcher's shop was twelve buildings away. I fairly leapt down the lane and ran to the back of the shop, up the stairs, where I banged on the midwife's door.

Her daughter answered. "Mama's been all night with the baker's wife." She squinted at the sunlight. "Should be home soon."

"Soon as she's back, tell her she's needed at the Stillbrookes' house, up the lane. It's"—what word had Mother used?—"dire."

I left the butcher's to go for Father, but I'd not gone far when I spotted the midwife just down the lane, trudging homeward, her apron splotched with blood. Before I could even hail her, a lad my age, maybe younger, whipped past Maudey and snatched her bag off her shoulder.

"For the love of God, you mongrel!" the midwife cried as he ran off down the street. "That satchel's got naught but my instruments!" She spotted me gaping. "You, boy! Chase that scoundrel down, won't you now?"

I sprinted after the thief and jumped on his back, knocking him to the dirt, but he held fast to the bag until I pummeled his hand with my fist and heard bones splinter.

The thief dropped the bag and raced away, howling and cradling his hand. I was left sick to my stomach with shame.

The midwife shuffled over and picked up her bag, eyeing me as if I were the one who'd robbed her. "What ill wind blew you to my door?"

"Did I not rescue thy bag for thee?"

"Well, la-di-dah," she muttered. "You with all your fancy *thee*s and *thy*s," and she started toward the butcher's rickety steps.

"Wait! Please, thee must come at once. My mother is hurting fiercely . . . many weeks too early."

"Can't you see I'm near dead tired? Find yourself another midwife," the ungrateful crone muttered.

"But none other will come to a Quaker house!" I shouted.

After a deep sigh, she wiped her face with her apron, turned around, and followed me home.

Next I dashed to the shipyard to find Father, but he was out on the river, water-testing the keel of a ship he'd helped to build. By the time he came ashore, two hours had passed since Mother had sent me rushing to Maudey's.

Grace greeted us at the door with terrified eyes, the midwife right behind her, wiping her hands on her soiled apron. I listened for the sound of a baby's wail or its cooing in Mother's arms. There was only silence.

The midwife said, "The both of 'em. Not even time to baptize the child—a girl, she was. Your wife gave her the name Matilde."

Crushed as he was, Father found his voice and dug some money out of a basket in the kitchen. "My children and I thank thee for thy services. Not to worry, good woman, we Quakers do not baptize. Our Matilde will find her way to Heaven eternally in the arms of her mother."

And so we buried the two in one grave.

But since that day, a sickening thought has wheedled its way into my mind a thousand-thousand times. I broke that boy's hand, and for nothing. His stomach was probably rumbling with hunger. No doubt he was after some money to bring a heel of bread, a bit of fruit, a sweetmeat home to his ailing mother, on the very day my own mother passed into eternity. No good came of my adding to his misery.

This I told no one, least of all Grace and Father.

Today, these memories flooded my mind when the men carried a flailing Dorothy away to jail. I tell myself she'll find solace in the arms of her own mother—until I remember that Sarah Good was taken to Boston and Dorothy will be held at Ipswich.

Miss Patience will never forgive me, nor will I forgive myself for letting those men take Dorothy away.

But even less can I forgive myself for the sickening sound of bones snapping like twigs.

Patience

At the next Lord's Day meeting, I'm still distraught over Dorothy and seething at the cowardice of the shoemaker's apprentice. Dorothy is not the only one who's been arrested recently, though. Goodwives Rebecca Nurse and Martha Corey have both been brought before the magistrates—both old and venerable ladies, Gospel women as far as any of us ever knew. Both proclaiming their innocence, both jailed like poor Dorothy. And still the afflicted girls are as restless and wrathful as ever. The list of victims grows with the list of bewitchers: the Proctors' maid Mary Warren, the Putnams' servant Mercy Lewis, and even Ann Putnam's mother are having fits now.

At least Abigail is calm beside me. Several of the other afflicted girls are writhing and raging in their pews despite all efforts to hush them.

Reverend Parris steps aside for our guest, Reverend Deodat Lawson. He was ours before Reverend Parris came to be our minister four years ago, and now he's returned for a visit, to offer his support in these trying times. Today he's been giving *very* long sermons, morning and afternoon. I wish Mother had let me bring sewing to keep me awake.

Reverend Lawson's words blur and fade in my mind, but they stir up the afflicted girls like the dasher paddle in a butter churn. "God, righteous and holy, would not afflict you without a cause," he says, looking at each of the girls in turn. "God has singled you out by giving liberty to Satan to range and rage amongst you."

I doubt they feel lucky to be chosen for such an honor, and to prove my guess, they're growing even more restless.

"Your sermon is too long!" shouts Betty Parris.

The rest of us hold back gasps of shock. *No one* interrupts a preaching minister. Not without paying a staggering fine. Perhaps Betty is more brazen because it's not her father preaching today.

"We cannot make sense of your text!" cries Abigail Williams, who swore a few days ago that she'd been choked and struck dumb by a witch. Well, there is nothing amiss with her voice now!

Good Reverend Lawson forges on, reminding us that we should pity the girls for their sufferings at Satan's hands.

All my life I've heard about Satan trapping the souls of God's saintly followers. Betty Parris has said Satan promised her that if she obeyed him, she'd go to a Golden City. Well, where *is* this Golden City? In New Hampshire? Virginia? Heaven? I suppose it is all a lie, one of the Devil's many false promises. Perhaps Satan has also claimed that in this Golden City, a mere girl may speak over an ordained minister when his words are not to her liking.

Chapter 12
April to May

Patience

Abigail's eyes are fixed on something in the distance, far out our window. "What is it you see, sister?" I ask her.

"The old woman, Prudence Blevins." She yanks me closer. "See? Right now there are two of her. Watch. A stronger one slides away from the bent and broken old body."

I gaze out the window and see only billowing white dogwood blossoms. "Oh, Abigail . . . could it not be your imagination?"

She turns hard, piercing eyes on me. "Why does no one believe me? Prudence Blevins is a witch!"

"The other witches all have more than one victim," says Mother, stirring a cauldron over the hearth fire. "Not a soul in Salem has a kind word to say about Goody Blevins, nor does she spare one for any of us—yet no others have come forward to say she's bewitched them. So why would she choose you alone, daughter? Why not the lot of us in this Gospel family? Why not Susannah Simms, who misses more Lord's Day meetings than she shows her face at? Or your sister, who's far more peevish than you are?"

"I am not!"

But Mother has asked a good question. The whole village is buzzing like cicadas, neighbor against neighbor. Two girls have testified against Rebecca Nurse, and a fair handful have named the brazen tavernkeeper Bridget Bishop and the wealthy Proctors. In fact, the Proctors' maid, who a fortnight ago was among the afflicted, now stands accused by four others of using witchcraft herself. Even little Dorothy Good has two accusers. But Goody Blevins? Only Abigail.

I can't get poor Dorothy out of my mind. The magistrates have examined her in prison—we know this much. They say she has spoken of the snake that sucks her finger, her familiar. She has named her mother as a witch and, Lord help us, she has confessed to witchly misdeeds of her own. Balderdash! The magistrates would've squeezed that confession out of her. They didn't allow spectators at her examination, so I can only imagine how they vexed and tormented the child until she gave them the answers they wanted. As for the girls who pointed their fingers at Dorothy in the first place—well, they're mistaken. They must be. If I age to be a withered crone, I shall never believe Dorothy capable of such crimes.

She is all alone in that Ipswich jail. And what awaits her next? The gallows?

I must get to her somehow and give her courage for whatever horrors lie ahead.

Thomas

Thunk. Clink. Thump. Goodman Cawley has a massive boot propped upside down on a metal stand, and he hammers stubby nails into the sole.

"For a customer, sir? I told you they'd come."

"Nah, it's my own boot. Worn to the quick."

For weeks the shoemaker has been teaching me what he can, letting me practice on a few boots that have been hammered and sewn and patched and polished a hundred times. I am oddly comfortable among the leather and pegs, the boar's hair needles, the greasy oils and pungent polishes of the shop. I have a real feel for leather—the look of it, the smell, the touch. Once I even tried chewing a piece, which left my jaw aching for two days.

But now we've finished our tasks for the day while the rabbit-skin glue sets on the shoes and boots. "No work here for one—twice as little for two. Apprentice, bah," Goodman Cawley grumbles. "Where's all the customers you promised, eh, boy?"

"I brought you a half dozen, sir," I remind him. I've marked them all down in Goodman Cawley's ledger. "And I've a few more dangling between yea and nay."

"I'm figuring on nay," he says, as gloomy as a summer rain. "Ach, get out. You're making me itch."

I lay down the mallet, studying his jowly smooth-shaven face and his small, sad eyes. Sad because he has no family left. I learned this from one of the potential customers I called on, for as Goodman Murdock said, Goodman Cawley is well known in Salem. His wife and children died one and all with smallpox. I suspect he's lonely and secretly enjoys my company, or at least enjoys having someone to spill his ill-tempered remarks on.

"Out with you now, boy. Give me an afternoon's peace, hear me?"

"Yes, sir."

So I go wandering on this windy spring day, with no particular place to go, and find myself at Gallows Hill. Perching on a giant rock, I let my eyes blur at waving grass in the distance. Up close are the cross-planks and the looped rope affixed to the top beam, designed for one thing only: to hang convicted witches, guilty or not.

Hearing footsteps behind me, I spin around to see someone about my age.

"Frightful sight, eh, up against that blue sky?" the boy says. He's much sturdier than I am, probably eats better. His yellowish hair sticks out every which way, including over his face. In front of me now, he rocks heels-to-toes on boots worn through the leather, which I can't help but notice. "I come up here every so often. You?"

"Never before. It's gruesome."

"To be sure!" He looks me up and down. "You're a Quaker, eh?"

I nod, accustomed to the term by now. "We call ourselves Friends. I'm Thomas Stillbrooke."

"Thatcher Cade's my name. Call me Thatch, like the straw on your roof." A large hand reaches out for mine. "I expect you've heard of my pa—he's a carpenter, like Jesus. We Cades are the best woodworkers in the Bay Colony. What's your pa do?"

My nose and throat stinging, I say, "He was a shipwright, but he's gone now. My mother too. I have a sister, though." Somehow it feels as if Grace isn't enough to call a family. I could never say *we Stillbrookes.*

"Sister, eh? Is she pretty?"

"I never noticed. She's my *sister.*"

"You'd notice if she looked like a bulldog. *My* sister does." He's framed by the gallows in the background, and when the wind stirs up, I imagine a body swaying in the brisk breeze.

I have to shake off that vision. "So," he says, "no pa, no ma. What do you do, then, to keep your sister fed?"

"I'm apprenticed to Goodman Cawley, the cordwainer."

Thrusting a holey boot up in the air, he says, "If there's anybody who needs a shoemaker, it's me, Thatcher Cade! My feet are growing faster than corn."

My eyes light up with promise of another good customer, and maybe my first friend.

"You boarding with Goodman Cawley, then?"

I shake my head. "We stay with a stingy widow who gives us a corner on the floor."

"What stingy widow is it?"

I hesitate. "Goodwidow Prudence Blevins."

"Ah, the old witch. Watch your britches with that one!"

"I've heard that a few times. But those boots—maybe you ought to come by Goodman Cawley's shop."

"Me and my pa just might," he says brightly. "If we can find the time. We've got more work than we can handle in the shop. This is Monday, isn't it? Goodwife Willowby gives lessons Mondays, so I come up here where the old fusspot can't find me."

"Why here? Why not hide in the forest or out on the bay where you could be just as invisible?"

He shrugs his broad shoulders. "Always liked this spot, or I used to before this spring." The wind whips through his haystack of hair. "Did I tell you my pa's a carpenter, like Jesus?"

"You did."

Thatch jerks his thumb over his shoulder, toward the gallows. "That back there behind me? My pa built it."

There is nothing I can say to this that my eyes don't already tell.

"Aye, it chills the blood, I know," he says.

The rope swings in the wind, which unsettles a rough wooden stool that totters on three legs below the gallows. Shuddering, I picture that stool being yanked away from the feet of Goody Sarah Good, and she with the rope tight around her neck.

Thatch is silent only a moment before he brightens. "Goodman Cawley's shop, you say? Perhaps I'll go there soon and see about that new pair of boots. Just make sure your old witch is nowhere nearby."

Chapter 13
June

Thomas

A law book as heavy as an anvil has come from Boston. I've saved my wages for this treasure, and I carry it with me whenever Goodman Cawley sends me out on an errand or when I go questing for customers. I make a point of passing through the market square that's thriving on these summer mornings, on my way to a quiet bench to study. Somehow no matter where I'm headed, I seem to pass by the fish stall.

She might be there.

Goodwife Woodstock has noticed my lingering nearby. "You, Quaker boy, have you nothing better to do?" She pulls a pale, lanky fish out of a bucket and waggles it in my direction. "Two pence. It'll feed a household."

Shaking my head, I hurry toward the Friends' meetinghouse behind the square, as though that's where I intended to go the whole time.

Patience

This is the day Mother goes to peddle our fish at the Ipswich market, so I ask to go along.

"No, you're needed here to mind our stall."

"Abigail can do that," I say dismissively. "Please, Mother. I've not been to Ipswich in months and months."

"It's just a little village. What's there that isn't here?" Mother asks, paddling a pot of oats that will, as usual, be more glue than gruel. I pray the honey pot is brimming to give the glue some zest.

"What's *there* is the jail where poor Dorothy Good is, all alone."

Mother spins round, dripping oatmeal from her paddle. "The witch's daughter! Lucky to get the cursed child out of our house before disaster befell us. Confessed, didn't she?"

"Nothing's proved against her yet, Mother. And she must be terrified, moldering in that jail." In the gossip whirling around Salem Village, I've heard harrowing stories of jail fever, of near-starvation, of vermin and filth. Sarah Osborne died in the Boston jail this very month, before her trial could commence. I doubt she's even had a proper burial in the one true faith.

Mother is not an unkind person—just a prickly one. She sighs. "I suppose you could come help me in Ipswich, but mind you, I'll expect you to truly help. Don't fancy that you can spend the whole day at the jail fluttering round that girl. Mark my words: if the mother is a witch, the child is a witch." She drops a dollop of gruel into one of our wooden bowls. "I do pity the baby, though."

"The baby?"

"Oh, yes," she says and leans over to whisper. "Sarah Good is heavy with child."

And is that child to be born in jail? What a horrible thought!

Thomas

"It's lavender, by the scent of it," Grace says, "though it's been nearly snuffed out by all the weedy growth." She yanks stalks of weeds from around a purplish plant and snaps off a posy, which she waves under my nose. "Now that I've scrubbed years of grime from this pigpen that's Goody Pru's house, I'll tuck bits of lavender here and there to keep it all smelling lovely."

I look my sister full in the face and see that she bears no resemblance to a bulldog, as Thatch claims his sister does. Grace is fair and slight, with wispy, nearly white hair and sad blue eyes and a nose that turns up a tick at the tip. I could close the circle of my thumb and middle finger around her small wrist. I suppose I shall someday have to find her a husband; who else is there to do it?

Were it not for Grace, I'd be eating poisonous mushrooms and bitter grasses and falling deathly ill. I've heard a man at the market speak of a strange substance that can work its way into the rye flour that ladies bake with. He said it might cause violent spasms or nightmare visions . . . much like the afflictions that've been marked as signs of witchcraft. But no one else has suggested such a possibility. Our neighbors are convinced of the Devil's hand in the misery.

More and more souls have become afflicted. More and more witches have been accused—men as well as women, many of them from neighboring towns. A few weeks ago, the authorities arrested someone as far away as Maine: Reverend George Burroughs, a minister who once served the Salem Village congregation. He is a learned man, a graduate of Harvard College, where I hope to study someday, and yet how far he's fallen. He's had some doings with the Wabanaki, signed a pact with them. Some say it's a Devil's pact. There's talk that he murdered two of his wives, though all anyone can say for certain is that he was cruel to them while they lived. People speak of his uncommon physical strength and call him the ringleader, even the king, of all the witches. At least a dozen accusers have come forward to say they've witnessed his evil deeds.

Soon the trials will begin, under a more proper court than the preliminary examinations. Judges and jurors are gathering from all over the countryside to decide who will go to Gallows Hill.

Now I follow Grace and her sprigs of lavender into the house, where Goody Pru has fallen asleep with her cheek on the table. She barely has the strength to walk from bed to board.

She no longer goes to the outhouse but relieves herself in a bucket that Grace tends to. God bless Grace; I couldn't do it.

✳

Goody Pru has entirely given up going to pray at the meetinghouse, which is why Reverend Parris has come calling on her this evening. She snaps awake as he sits on the bench opposite her one chair, while Grace and I are sentinels standing behind her.

"Goodwidow Blevins," he says, holding a cup of Grace's comfrey tea, "we have noticed that you've absented yourself from our congregation of late."

Goody Pru looks through the slits of her eyes. It's hard for her to keep them open after supper. She's usually snoring long before dark, and she has a mighty snore. Reverend Parris leans forward to make out her thin voice.

"Didn't think anybody would notice, concentrating as your whole flock does on the Good Word."

Grace smiles at the familiar surliness behind Goody Pru's sugarcoated words.

"Eh-hmm, to be sure," says Reverend Parris, "but we take note when one of our members isn't among us on the Lord's Day." With his cup in front of his face, he pauses. I believe he has more to say but isn't sure how to say it.

Goody Pru's not about to let him hide behind his tea. "You suspect, good Reverend Parris, that I've quit worship because I've been cavorting with the Devil? Do I tell it straight?"

A swig of tea gurgles down the minister's throat, else he'd spit it across the table. "Well, Goodwidow Blevins, how would you answer such a charge?"

I hold my breath waiting for her reply, but Grace is kinder than I am, and a rescuer besides. With a half curtsey, she says, "Good Reverend Parris, you can see how poorly Goody Blevins is—weak as a newborn." To demonstrate, she lifts Goody's arm off the table, and when she lets go, it thuds on the rough wood. "See, sir?"

Goody Pru turns to her with a gap-toothed stare, her face sliding into her loose bonnet so only one eye is visible to the minister. A cyclops. "Surely, I am a witch. I drag my body all over Salem casting evil spells on innocent girls. Just look at this child here. Doesn't she seem to be besotted and bewitched? Hmm?"

The good reverend looks perplexed—eager to believe he's hearing an earnest confession, but puzzled by Pru's tone.

"She's hot and cold with fever too, Reverend," says Grace. "Speaking nonsense."

But Pru brushes away Grace's efforts. "As sure as I'm breathing," she croaks, her one visible eye sliding left and right, "I'm the bride of Lucifer, the mother of Beelzebub."

Grace tries a different strategy. "Has your tea gone cold, Reverend?" That's her way of saying, *thank you and goodbye.*

There's a glint in Goody Pru's eyes now. "Aye, how brave you are, Reverend, to drink my fine herb tea. Leaves of night-shade, is it, Grace?"

As much as Grace wants to see the good reverend gone from us, she just smiles sweetly and won't lie that the tea is steeping with poison. But the mere suggestion is enough to send Reverend Parris rushing out the door.

Chapter 14
June

Patience

In the midnight-black of the Ipswich jail, dark and cold as a cave, I'm aware of the rancid stink around me. Where do all these women relieve themselves? Dorothy must be lying in her own waste. This is unforgiveable.

The women are bellowing: "We demand light! It's the last God-given dignity we're allowed!"

I sense the guard feeling his way back along the oozing wall—to return with another lantern, I hope—while I try to stand directly in the middle of the passageway. I can feel the fetid air move as women peer through the bars of the cell doors on both sides of me. They jostle one another with arms thrust out, reaching for me, begging for food, blankets, tobacco.

"Sister, please, a comb or brush!" That one rakes her hands through a tangled nest of hair.

"Generous sister, have you any tooth powder? A thimbleful of rum?"

This is a nightmare darker than any I've ever suffered. Trembling with the horror of it, I tuck the hem of my skirt about me and run back up the stone steps, the clatter of my shoes echoing through the grim corridor. Clear air—I must have air, light.

Inhaling my fill, I'm immediately beset with guilt that I am allowed to escape, while those inside are condemned to stay. Something must be done for them. Something. So, I return to the dungeon below and search for the cell where the guard said I'd find Dorothy.

"I beg you, young miss, give me your shoes!" cries an old woman. "So cold on this floor, and my feet throb so."

"Rope! Enough to hang myself! Have a heart, good sister!"

All these women are accused witches? I had no idea there were so many here in Massachusetts. My stomach churns at their pathetic wants, their shrieks of anguish. How much longer can someone as frail as Dorothy Good survive these horrid conditions?

How much longer can I stand to be here, even free?

Thomas

I'm alone in the shop this afternoon. Goodman Cawley has been beckoned to the kitchen of Goodwife Mulberry, whose toothache has swollen her face to twice its size. The sturdy pliers we shoemakers use are perfect for pulling troublesome teeth. I'm not yet schooled in this art, and I'm in no hurry to practice it. I'm content with shoes and boots. They don't cry out when you stretch leather across them with those same pliers, though sometimes the pliers are still wet or crusted with blood from a sufferer's mouth.

I'm pounding a sheet of leather flat on my lapstone, three blows with the metal mallet and three with the wooden mallet, just as Goodman Cawley taught me. He insists on three and three, and if I accidentally land a fourth blow, he hollers at me.

The door swings open, butted by my new friend, Thatch. "It's Goodwife Willowby's lessons day, so I'm hiding out. Don't guess she or my pa would look for me here."

I hope he's brought some of his father's money. "Come, sit on this stool. I'll measure your feet with the sizing stick."

"I've not come to buy shoes today."

"Maybe not, but if my master comes in, I ought to look industrious."

Thatch toes off one shoe—a well-made shoe, though it's been stretched past its limit—and slips his foot onto the stick. I've grown used to the smell of other people's feet the same way a dog gets accustomed to the stink of rotten meat.

"You're a medium."

"Medium, plain ordinary," he complains, and I don't blame him. If we could be more precise, our shoes would fit so much more comfortably. I'll have to talk to Goodman Cawley about that.

"Been back to Gallows Hill?" Thatch asks.

"Not since the day we met there."

"It'll soon be put to use, the new gallows will. For Bridget Bishop. This isn't her first time round as a witch, you know. My pa says ten, twelve years ago she was accused and found innocent, but here she is on the docket again. I was at her trial this morning. You missed all the sport, Thomas."

As much *sport* as Sarah Good's examination? "I'll have to settle for your account." I get up to check on the sole leather softening up in a bucket of water.

Thatch hops around to jam his foot back into his shoe. "The judges asked the usual questions." He lowers his voice in imitation. "'Goody Bishop, what contract have you made with the Devil? Why have you not a heart to confess the truth?'" Pitching his voice high and shrill, he gives Goody Bishop's response: "'I am innocent. I know nothing of it. I am no witch. I know not what a witch is.'"

"Do any of us?" I go over to rearrange the shoe forms. Goodman Cawley never seems to notice when they're hanging on the wrong hooks, which happens now that we have some customers.

Thatch says, "Well, the judges said, 'If you know not what a witch is, how do you know you're not one?' A dozen people looked Goody Bishop straight in the eye and accused her. One goodman testified that she sold him a bewitched pig, and more than one accused her of murder. Said she'd bewitched two or three children and at least four grown people to death! And then there was blather about those poppets they found hidden in her walls."

"Poppets?"

"Made of rags and hog bristles and bits of lace. They say Goody Bishop sticks needles and pins into 'em, and girls six houses away feel it, like they're being impaled in those same spots."

I fish out the sodden leather from the bucket, wringing it as dry as I can.

"And they're swearing she's bewitched horses, even pigs. Now, what would the Devil want with our livestock?"

Thatch has a knack for coaxing laughter out of me. I ask, "Do you believe she's innocent?"

"I want to because I miss her raucous cider parties. She'd press apples out of her own orchard, and my friends and I, we'd slurp down that cider on many a spring night. Then, full up, we'd piss off a bridge and stumble home before dawn. Our fathers never knew we were gone. Before you were here."

If I had been here, would I have been among Thatch's friends at Goody Bishop's house late into the night, drinking spirits? No! But maybe? I blink the thought away. "I asked you, Thatch, do you believe she's not a witch?"

"It makes no difference, do I or don't I. She's headed for Gallows Hill. Execution's set for next week, the tenth of June. Come watch with me. Everyone'll be in a merry mood. It'll be like a bonfire night."

The idea sours my stomach, and I soothe it by sniffing a piece of soft cowhide. "No, I've no appetite for a hanging."

Thatch's shoulders stiffen, and I wonder if he thinks I'm a coward or a milksop, but he says soberly, "Nor have I, truth be told. But I have to be there to help test the equipment—the cross bars, the ladder, the stool, all of it that my pa built. Ready to fix any of it that don't work, so Goody Bishop's end isn't as slow and miserable as it could be."

We're silent for a while, and I take up the lapstone—one, two, three, metal; one, two, three, wooden—until Thatch says, "Maybe you're the lucky one, Thomas Stillbrooke. You have no father to lead you into the bloody work of this world."

Patience

A bedraggled child's unblinking eyes gaze at me from a dark corner of the cell. Here is Dorothy Good, silent and alone.

"Dorothy—little one, it's me, Patience. Come closer so I can see you better." Neither my comforting voice nor my wiggling fingers through the bars draw her to the front of the cell.

A guard parades past the row of cells, shrugging off the women's filthy, outstretched hands.

I clench my teeth against a globule of rage. "Kind sir, could you shine your lantern into this child's cell so I can see her more clearly? Please," I add, hearing Mother's warning that we must always be polite, even to brutes such as he.

He flings his lantern chain in the general direction of the cell for just a moment before he turns away.

Stuffing down my fury, I fix my eyes on Dorothy again. I cover the tremor in my voice by lifting it into a singsong pitch, as if I'm crooning a lullaby: "Be brave, sweet Dorothy. Someone will come, will come to help soon." My voice growing stronger, I promise her: "I'll talk to my mother and father, to the magistrates, to your own father." What kind of a man is William Good that he's likely not even visited her?

The voice of a woman in the cell across from Dorothy's rises above the others. She reeks, so I try to keep a goodly distance. But her long arm thrusts out to graze my sleeve.

"Young miss, I am not so bold as to ask for your lovely cloak." Still, she gives it a vicious twist, as if to wrench it off my shoulders. It's tied tight beneath my chin, and the knot holds firm. "But I beg of you, give me your apron, your bonnet, anything I can lay over my weary bones."

What am I to do? So many of them, guilty or not, all so desperate. I give her my cloak. But immediately three other women lurch forward to grab it, pulling at it until so fiercely I hear the fabric rip. It'll soon be in shreds.

The cold I feel without it seeps up from my bones, even in early June.

A different guard comes, swinging a lantern in each hand, and the shouting settles down. Now I see well into Dorothy's cell. She lies shivering in a puddle of God knows what substance. Her hair is matted and snarled and, oh! Something crawls up her cheek and into her scalp. Fleas? Lice? Her lips are swollen and cracked, her dress riddled with holes from the rats—the only creatures growing fat in the jail.

The guard looks away as Dorothy squints in the dim light. And now I see why she will not come closer to me. Around her ankle, screwed into the dirt floor, is a leg iron.

Chapter 15
June

Patience

Business is slow at the Ipswich market, so Mother's needle and thread whip in and out of Father's tattered winter breeches. Without looking up from her work, she sniffs the air. "You've got the stench of the jail on you, daughter. You've seen the child?"

"Oh, it breaks my heart."

"If your heart needs breaking, look to your afflicted sister. No end of it with that one. First she says Sarah Good bewitched her, now she says it's Prudence Blevins." She jabs an elbow toward a bucket of cod and squints at the sky. "They'll bake in this summer sun, and who'll buy from me then? Pah, might as well pack up and go home."

Back home we go, our wheels grinding slowly over the rugged, rocky ground until my insides are so shaken that I'm sure my teeth will come loose before the first thatched roof of Salem pops into view.

*

Father comes into the house waving a large striped bass, which Mother grabs and places on the gutting board. "Treasures like this one are running thick and fast today," Father says with uncommon mirth.

It's a good time to ask him about Dorothy, to the tune of Mother snipping silver scales from the bass. "Father, I've been to the Ipswich jail. Dorothy Good is held in irons there, filthy and reeking of her own waste."

Father's good mood turns sour as fast as a spinning wheel whirls. "She's the child of a witch, a confessed witch herself. You think our Lord has age restrictions on witchery?"

"But surely she is young enough to be redeemed, Father. And she is suffering so. Couldn't you speak to our constables and find out if anything can be done to get her released?"

Mother says, "Hrumph," and she and Father exchange looks until he settles the matter: "Don't ask me. It's in God's hands."

So I go to Reverend Parris's house to talk to the man who talks directly to the Lord.

As I approach the parsonage, where this madness all began five months ago, my eyes are drawn to the pasture behind it, thick with new green grass. A rabbit darts out of a bush, sees me intruding, and hurries into protective cover. The large red maple that commands one corner of the pasture is budding now, and I picture it full and ablaze in the fall. All here is so peaceful and lush. How could works of evil happen in such a place?

Inside the house, I find Reverend Parris in the little room he uses as his office. His white sleeves are rolled up to the elbow as he wipes the small squares of glass in his window. How unbefitting of a minister! But I suppose with Tituba locked up and the other women of his household all afflicted by witchcraft—including his wife now—he must manage some tasks for himself.

"Good Reverend Parris," I begin with a curtsey, "I've come to talk to you about a child in our flock."

Reverend Parris rolls his sleeves back to his wrists. "What child, young Miss Patience? Your afflicted sister?"

"It's little Dorothy Good, sir. She is held in irons in a filthy cell in Ipswich, with no one to care for her. Can she not be released and raised in Godliness?"

Reverend Parris is a man who thinks long before he utters a word, unlike myself.

Patience. Why was I cursed with this name? I have so little of it left right now. "May I, sir?" I reach and he willingly gives me the rag. More vigorously than I'd work at home, I polish the window panes.

Three squares of glass later, he says, so quietly and calmly: "We are either saints or devils. The scripture gives us no middling state. Plain and simple, the child is a witch and deserving of her punishment."

"Oh, sir, I think not!" I feel my face burn, speaking so boldly to a minister, but despite his frown, I can't stop. "If she does have powers, she has only used them to save herself! That is good conjuring, white magic, like the healing herbs my mother uses, not the Devil's work." So what of the familiar beneath Dorothy's chair, the unseen snake that sucks between her tiny fingers, or so she says? And the strange look on her countenance when she bit off that doll's eyes and tossed them at Abigail? The more I ponder it, the less I know for sure.

As if Reverend Parris reads my mind, he says, "Countermagic, my child, even used against the Great Deceiver, is just as perfidious as witchcraft."

My mouth runs dry. In my fury, I've polished the window so hard that it squeaks. All these rules, all these pronouncements—to what end? How does Dorothy's suffering benefit our village? Locking her away, starving her, shunning her—how does any of it bring the rest of us closer to God's grace?

"Witch or not, sir, Dorothy is a child of not even five years. A lifetime spans ahead of her. Can she not be led to make her peace with God?"

He pauses again before answering.

I quickly fill the silence. "Guided by your firm hand, of course, kind Reverend Parris." Flattery cannot hurt.

But he is unmoved. "She shall be judged, Miss Patience. It is not our place to interfere with the judgment of our great and blessed God."

Chapter 16
June

Thomas

Goodwife Bridget Bishop has been condemned to die this day, Tuesday, the tenth of June. The marketplace is nearly deserted. Everyone's at the hanging—everyone but Patience Woodstock, who's minding her family's fish stall. There will surely be a hungry crowd returning home after the execution.

"Good day, Miss Patience," I shyly offer.

"I would not call it a good day, Thomas Stillbrooke." She jerks her head toward Gallows Hill. Even from this distance, we can hear the hum of the crowd. "Do you wonder about Goodwife Bishop's final thoughts as the wagon bumped along the road up there?"

Not knowing what to say, I keep silent.

"Well, *I* wonder, if you don't. My mother and father and sister are all there, along with the rest of Salem. Why not you?"

The faithful Friends among us stand staunchly opposed to hangings, public spectacle hangings especially, but I simply answer, "I would rather not witness this sad event."

Her eyes flash. "And what of the other horrors afoot? Dorothy Good, the child you let the constables carry away . . ."

"I haven't forgotten her," I say quietly.

"Well then, will you turn your eyes away from her suffering? You should see the squalor of her cell, the filth and stench and vermin, the leg iron and her empty eyes. She will not speak even a word. Will you turn away from all that, Thomas?"

I draw myself up. "Of course not, Miss Patience."

Patience

I'm sorely vexed over Dorothy, as I tried to explain to Thomas Stillbrooke this morning, but that is not my only worry. Abigail has been growing even worse in mind and body. God only knows where her soul is.

Mother has given her herbs and roots and healing teas of every taste and color, but Abigail has taken to spitting them out and shouting vile words.

After she and Mother return from Bridget Bishop's hanging, she ranges about the house, striking out with her arms or else pulling at her hair, cursing Mother and me when we come close. Finally she falls into an exhausted sleep on the floor in front of the cold hearth.

Mother mutters, "How shall we find a husband for you, Patience, when our home is beset with an addle-brained sister?"

"I shall find my own husband. But not soon," I retort.

"Nonsense. We must see to it that you wed a decent man who can bring home a goodly living. It's hopeless for this one," she adds, pointing to Abigail splayed out gracelessly on the floor.

Curious . . . . Why has Abigail been the one to suffer when I am left free? Oh, not that I wish to be screaming and writing on the floor in a fit, head wrenched until I'm nearly seeing what's behind me. But I wonder why I've escaped the afflictions. It occurs to me that I may not be virtuous enough. Perhaps Satan only wants to capture the truest saints among us and not the—well, how would I describe myself? One who lags behind.

Mother yanks Abigail's shift down to cover her heels. "I suppose we shall have to sneak good Dr. Griggs in before your father comes home, but how shall we pay?"

I look at my poor sister, at peace in her sleep, and wonder if she is bewitched or out of her wits. There is no easy remedy for either.

Thomas

Pretending that I'm speaking to no one more important than Sawtucket the beggar, I stand in front of Magistrate Corwin's desk. "Sir, I am Thomas Stillbrooke. I've come to speak to you about a child held in jail under inhumane conditions."

Magistrate Corwin parts a stack of papers and books, one much like my own law book, to see me better. "Ah, you. The Quaker boy. I know of no Quaker child in our custody. This child is kin to you?"

"No, sir, a neighbor of a friend." Is Patience Woodstock a friend? "The child's name is Dorothy Good, sir."

"Daughter of William, who is a good-for-nothing wastrel, and Sarah, who awaits trial as a witch? Quite a heritage, wouldn't you say?"

I say nothing.

"The child has confessed to witchcraft, boy."

"So has the maid Mary Warren, sir, and she's been released from jail."

Corwin waves a dismissive hand. "The circumstances were different."

Indeed they were. First Mary Warren had fits like the other afflicted girls. But her master, Goodman Proctor, said she was feigning her suffering and declared that he'd beat it out of her. In April, Mary claimed she was cured—and the other girls named *her* as a witch.

"Mary Warren cooperated with the authorities and helped us identify several other witches, including the Proctors," Corwin says. "Dorothy Good has been no help to us, except to name her mother as a witch, and this we already knew."

"With all due respect, sir, may I read the record of Dorothy Good's interrogation?"

"No, you may not."

I show him my book. "I am studying the law, sir."

He laughs while I stand soberly before him. "Do you not see my table groaning under the weight of so many court documents? Begone, Thomas Stillbrooke. Come back to me when you're twenty-five, or send your father to me."

"I have no father, sir, and Dorothy won't survive until I'm twenty-five."

But I've already lost his ear, and his eyes have turned back to the papers cluttering his desk.

Patience

When the doctor arrives, he wakes Abigail. She's as docile as a kitten now. The fit has passed as mysteriously as it came upon her.

Mother describes it all, sparing Abigail no embarrassment. "Thrashing about on the floor like an apoplectic she-wolf, shouting curses that would curdle Reverend Parris's blood and summon the Devil himself to a black supper."

Dr. Griggs looks into Abigail's eyes and up her nose, feels the skin of her arm—"Icy," he proclaims—and asks for a sample of her water.

"What?" Abigail shouts indignantly.

Mother snaps, "I don't save it up when she passes water. What do you need it for?"

Dr. Griggs opens the gaping mouth of his wooden tool box to reveal terrifying instruments for probing and stabbing and slicing. Abigail shudders and turns away.

"I can study the urine for smell and consistency and color and morbific matter. That is the best way to determine if her humours are out of balance."

I wonder which of Abigail's humours—yellow bile, black bile, blood, or phlegm—could be causing these fits.

Suddenly Abigail sits up, knocking his arm away. "I am not sick! I've been bewitched! *She's* causing it!"

The doctor's eyes snap toward me. "Your sister?"

Me!

"No, Prudence Blevins!" says Abigail. "The witch pulls me ever closer to the Devil, and when I resist, she tortures me. Nearly choked me this morning, and last night she drew me to the fire in Reverend Parris's pasture. I would've been charred to ash if Tituba hadn't pulled me away."

Mother's eyebrows fly to the top of her forehead. "Tituba's still in jail, daughter."

"Her specter, then," Abigail says quickly. "See my face? It's burnt nearly crisp!"

Mother kneels and wraps her arms around Abigail. "No, daughter, your face is as pale as muslin." But at that very moment, Abigail's countenance reddens such as mine does when I've lingered too long gathering herbs in the noonday sun.

Dr. Griggs looks as shocked as Mother and I are. He snaps his box shut and announces, "She shall have to be bled to right the balance. I must go home and collect the leeches. They can suck three times their body weight of bad blood, you know."

"NO!" Abigail shouts.

Mother sighs. "Doctor, I'll not have those creatures on my child's body if she herself declares it will do her no good. We'll deal with this our own way."

"And what's to be done about that evil witch Blevins?" cries Abigail. "Tell me that, good doctor!"

Mother gets to her feet and leads the doctor to the door. "Good day," she says, as a gust of wind blows the doctor's hat off into our kitchen garden, where it settles among the turnips and parsnips and leaves the rosy tomatoes untouched.

Chapter 17
June

Thomas

"Thee looks so pale, sister. What's amiss?"

Grace is curled up in her bedroll in the corner, even in the daylight. These last few weeks since Bridget Bishop went to Gallows Hill have tried everyone's nerves. Yesterday I pressed so hard upon a piece of leather that I broke the knife clean in half, and when I tossed the blade away outside the shop, a passing girl shrieked at the sight. The whole town is stretched taut with tension. But I've rarely seen Grace so still and wan.

"Don't trifle with her," Pru says. "She has the ague."

Yes, she suffers from a fever, as well as a listlessness so unlike my industrious sister. Is this the first sign of her becoming afflicted like so many other girls her age? Afflicted by witchcraft? I don't want to think it, but my mind jumps to the rumors that Prudence Blevins is a witch.

Pru, it seems, has rallied her energy to care for Grace. She's brewed tea and poured a mugful of it, offering it to Grace. With a shaky hand, Grace takes it. Suddenly suspicious, I snatch the mug away from my sister, sniff its pungent aroma, and suck a drop of tea off my finger. I am not struck dead on the spot, but

I set the mug on the table, out of Grace's reach, for the time being.

"Stand away," Pru snaps. "Tonight she must take a hammer and wait in the forest. Listen for the clock. At the first stroke of midnight—"

"Pru!" I blurt out. "This is ridiculous."

"Ach, not a word, boy. Well do I know what's the cure for the ague. Passed from grandmother to mother to daughter."

"Grace is not your daughter!"

Goody Pru's small eyes burn into mine. "You think I need to be told? A daughter has never been my lot in life. Neither a son."

Grace whispers, "Perhaps that's why she took us in."

"Don't speak behind my back! Lord knows, you two conniving urchins are no replacement for what I never had."

"We mean no disrespect, Goody Pru," I say. To draw her away from her absurd cure for Grace's fever, I ask, "Have you no family at all, then?"

An impertinent question, but she doesn't snipe at me this time. "None, not since my mother died." She pauses, as if considering what more to say. "Alice, my mother's name was—she was one of the cunning folk. Knew all the ways of the world. Knew the moon like it was her own heart waxing and waning, knew when to plant root crops or slaughter a sow, knew just what plants could heal you—or kill you when sickness came on the hand of Satan. That sort of knowing ordinary folks don't have."

"But you do?" I ask skeptically.

"Not like Alice. She could read the future, my mother could. Warned me not to take Obadiah Blevins for a husband. That no-good wastrel gave me a baby what never let out a peep, dead before I even set a foot on the floor beside the bed."

"Oh, how you must've grieved, Goody Pru," Grace murmurs.

"Well, I lived through it, didn't I? That night, Alice dug a grave and we buried the shriveled thing out back behind the privy. I was feverish for three days. Alice waited to die till my milk dried up."

Grace says, "We also lost a baby and our mother together."

My eye catches Grace's, and I know we're both remembering how it felt to leave behind the double grave when we sailed across the world—and Father's watery grave between there and here. Shaking off the memory, I ask, "What became of Goodman Blevins?"

"*Good*man, you call him, boy? Ha! Took off before sundown and never showed his pocked face again." She leans back and lifts the hammer. "Motherless, husbandless, and penniless I was, and barren as a nun. A woman gets old fast that way."

And she does not pretend otherwise. Perhaps it's this—her undisguised sorrow, twisted into bitterness—that frightens her neighbors, far more than any witchcraft she may or may not be using.

"Now, don't you go pitying me!" Pru snaps. "God sends us sufferings according to our sins. Just do as I say, girl. When the clock strikes midnight, you must take this hammer and stoop to pound a large nail into the ground till naught but its head sticks up. Hear me well?"

"Yes, Goody Pru," Grace replies, her voice weak and hoarse, to satisfy the old woman, though I know she has no intention of doing as Pru says.

Pru's drooping eyelids now leave only slits for her raisin-black eyes to bore into me. "Must be done afore the twelfth stroke, or it won't work."

Does this not sound like witchcraft? But if it is meant to

heal Grace—if it is meant for good—then can it really be called the Devil's work?

I've no time to ponder further. Sarah Good and four others are to stand trial today, and I mean to be there and see what becomes of poor little Dorothy Good's mother.

*

The case is heard before a court of nine judges, including Hathorne and Corwin, and a great number of jurors as well. Sarah Good is brought before them all, her clothes in rags, her face looking ancient, though I've heard she's not yet forty. Her accusers are there again to face her. I see Miss Abigail Woodstock among them and look for Miss Patience, but if she is here with her sister I can't spot her.

A curdling scream silences the crowd, then stirs it furiously. One of the afflicted girls cries, "Help me! I'm being stabbed! The apparition of Goody Good is stabbing me over and over!"

Two yeomen grab the arms of Goody Good until she's immobilized, but the stricken girl continues screaming: "Aye, aye, I'm dying! She's stabbing me!" A third yeoman finds a broken knife on the girl's lap. A knife I recognize.

The blade is carried to the magistrates' table. Magistrate Hathorne glares at Sarah Good, and that expression in itself is a silent sentence to hang her.

I step forward. "Sirs, I am Thomas Stillbrooke—"

"The lad who would not sign the oath," Magistrate Hathorne mutters.

"True, sir, but also true is the fact that I broke this knife on toughened shoe leather yesterday." I motion toward the girl as I take the knife handle from my breeches pocket. "This girl who claims she's been stabbed with it was there when I cast the blade into the briars." I take the accusation no further, but the meaning is clear: the girl picked up the blade of the knife herself and is telling a lie.

Magistrate Hathorne examines the matching knife halves and grimly says, "Young miss, you must never lie in a court of inquiry."

And *still* Sarah Good is declared guilty.

Her sentence is pronounced: she shall be hanged by the neck until dead, on Gallows Hill, on the nineteenth of July. I see Miss Abigail Woodstock across the room, overjoyed and dancing with the other victims, including the one with the knife, who has miraculously recovered from her stab wounds.

Chapter 18
June

Patience

We Woodstocks gather in a circle in front of the hearth, with Ruff at Father's feet, for our customary Bible lesson in the evening light.

Father reads to us from Isaiah with frightening gusto. *"When you pass through the waters, I will be with you; and when you pass through the rivers, they will not sweep over you . . ."*

I feel soggy just thinking of it. My mind wanders to Sarah Good's ghastly trial and to the others that followed it. Four other women are condemned to die with Goody Good. Even Rebecca Nurse, who's always seemed so pious and has been held in such esteem, will go to Gallows Hill. Tituba is spared for now, perhaps because she was so forthcoming with the magistrates from the beginning. Or perhaps because Reverend Parris wants her spared, as she's his property.

"When you walk through the fire, you will not be burned; the flames will not set you ablaze . . ." Father roars.

Mother and I both look at Abigail, whose face is serene, unburnt—her bewitching afflictions past, please God. Or have they merely *passed*, only to return when we least expect them?

"Daughter." Father's look my way is stern as the pages of the Bible flutter closed.

"Amen," I say hastily.

Most evenings, this is when Father goes to sleep, so that he can wake hours before first light when the fish run. The rest of us always sigh in relief when we hear him settle into his bed, making the ropes groan, and again when his snores rock our house. But now he puts the Bible on the high shelf over the hearth and says, "So, I'll stop in the privy, then be off. Don't know when I'll be home."

"Husband, I beg you, do not go!"

What is this? Father's word is law in our house; Mother almost never steps in.

"I must go, Bethia. Duty calls me."

"You mean to tell me Joseph Herrick can't conduct an arrest on his own? He should need no help to subdue a wretched old crone, half-blind and bent nearly in two. A burly, quick-fisted man like that! They say he takes a switch to his wife, and his daughters fare no better."

"Pay no heed to the gossipmongers," Father says, smashing his hat onto his balding head.

"Is it not *all* gossip, husband? Is it not gossip that sends you to capture a poor old woman, a penniless widow?"

"A witch," Father hisses. "And we have our own child's word against her. Do you not believe that Abigail is tormented?"

I cast a nervous glance toward Abigail, but she appears not to hear the conversation. Her eyes are on some distant shore.

"By Sarah Good, aye," Mother whispers. "We know of Sarah Good's wickedness. But when did Goodwidow Blevins do any of us harm? And why should she begin now?"

Father scoffs. "Herrick is arresting her tonight, and I will be there to see to it that she does not escape through some demonic trickery."

Mother turns her back to him and crosses her arms over her bodice. And Father's gone.

So Goodwidow Blevins is to be arrested. Perhaps now Abigail's torments will finally stop and life in our house will be peaceful again. That is, if Prudence Blevins actually is a witch, and the very witch afflicting my sister. There could be others. There's no shortage of witches hereabouts.

And what of Thomas Stillbrooke, who lives under Goody Blevins's roof? Will he be hauled off to jail as well? Oh, mercy! If I run all the way, perhaps I can get there in time to warn him.

Warn him to do *what*? He wouldn't lift a hand to save Dorothy, so what could he do to hold off my father and Constable Herrick now? If he tried to reason with them, they'd laugh in his face. If he tried to fight them—which he surely never would—they'd flatten him. And if he fled, they would catch him.

I can be of no use to him, but neither can I sit here at home and put the matter out of my mind.

"Mother, it's such a lovely evening, and I don't have a mind for spinning tonight . . ."

"Do you ever?" Mother mutters.

I sigh. "Tomorrow. But for now, might I take a walk? I promise to recite psalms all the way so no harm can come to me."

Mother, lost in her own reflections, is furiously rolling berry-juice-dyed yarn. "Mind you're home by dark," she says.

Unseen, I follow Father all the way to Prudence Blevins's house. Thomas Stillbrooke's house.

✳

A tree as wide around as a barrel, across the lane from the good-widow's time-worn hut, hides me well. Goodman Herrick's fist pounds on the door, which buckles a bit with the blows. No one answers for the longest time. At last Thomas Stillbrooke opens the door, and the two men shove their way inside, even as Thomas spreads his arms wide as a wall, shielding anyone inside.

I was mistaken to call Thomas a coward. He aims to protect Goodwidow Blevins as best he can. But he is only one boy, with the full power of God and the law bearing down upon him.

Thomas

Three resounding pounds on the door have jarred me to attention. I've opened it to find two men.

"I am Joseph Herrick," says the one I recognize, the constable who snatched Dorothy Good. "I've come for Goodwidow Prudence Blevins."

My eye flies to the law book tucked onto the shelf. For direction? Or, God help me, as a weapon? "On what legal charge, Goodman Herrick?"

"There are serious accusations against her."

Pru's breathing is labored and wheezy behind me. I know I am powerless to protect her against the men who've come for her. And Grace is mending from her illness but still too weak to stand with me against these intruders.

For courage, I listen to my memory of Father's words when two men with guns burst into our quiet London meetinghouse one First Day. I was a child, maybe seven years, and Grace but five, sheltering under the wing of Mother's cloak. I watched the angry men framed by the sunlight beyond the door they'd just burst through.

"We come in the name of the Church of England to put an end to your heresy once and forever." The man who spoke raised his gun. There were gasps as he shot a hole in the ceiling. Wood and plaster rained down upon us. The women and children bunched in a corner, but I stood with Father, clutching his hand—though I don't know if it was bravery or cowardice that kept me close to him.

"Welcome, friends," my father said, brushing the ceiling dust off his topcoat.

The ruffian who'd shot the hole stared at Father curiously—caught off-guard, perhaps, by his iron will. And perhaps realizing that having already fired his gun, he would need time to reload it before he could shoot again, though of course the other man still had a weapon at the ready.

Father returned the man's stare. "Friends, if thee will set down thy weapons, we can talk to one another man-to-man, but we cannot talk man-to-muzzle. Thee must both be weary, fighting heresy diligently for so many years. Won't thee come and have a seat among our men, and we shall discuss what God calls each of us to do?"

The intruders looked at one another in confusion, each waiting for the other to take action. Finally, the one who'd already fired his gun turned and left, and the other followed his boot prints in the dust. Father closed the door behind them. One of our women found a broom to sweep the fallen wood and plaster into a corner, and we took our seats on the benches and quietly resumed our meeting. I wondered then, and many times since, what would have happened if the men had come to sit among us, with their guns across their knees. I never let myself imagine the outcome if Father had not persuaded them to go in peace.

Now, I motion for Grace and Pru to move to the farthest dark corner of the house, which is to say no more than three feet from the men. They huddle together, each wrapped in a blanket.

"Good sirs." I swallow a plug of fear in my throat. "There has been some mistake."

"No mistake," scoffs the larger of the two men. I've seen his face, but I cannot put a name to it. He points to Goody Pru. "That old hag, she's a known agent of the Devil. A witch if ever there was one. You can tell by the stench of her."

Summoning my father's strength, I say, "Sir, that is the stench of age and poverty. With respect, I ask you to look at her. She's old and withered. Why, she could be your grandmother. You would seize this ancient, bent woman and throw her into your jail?"

The larger man opens up Pru's cupboard and rifles through the contents. Searching for signs of witchcraft, I suppose. "My own daughter Abigail has been tortured by Prudence Blevins, over and again. Saw it with my own two eyes."

Abigail? The sister of Patience? A common name, but she did claim that Pru had bewitched her. Is this man Patience's father, then? "Sir, did you see Goodwidow Blevins's hand upon your daughter?"

"Good as," he mutters, leaving the cupboard ajar and moving to the bed. He pulls the quilt off, lifts the straw-stuffed mattress to peer at the ropes stretched across the frame, kneels down to look at the dust beneath.

"But with due respect, I ask you again, sir, have you actually seen Goodwidow Prudence in the flesh doing harm to your daughter?" I point over my shoulder. "See how frail the woman is? Not strong enough to lift a foot and bring it down on a beetle without tottering to her knees."

Ignoring me, he kicks at Grace's and my bedrolls, checking for anything hidden under them.

Herrick says to me, "If not Prudence Blevins in the living flesh, then her apparition. She's a witch. We'll put an end to it."

Witch or not, there is good in her. She's given us a roof over our heads, and we've become an odd sort of family. "I will not let you take her!"

Goodman Herrick's face contorts. "I am an official representative of William and Mary, king and queen of all England. And you, boy, are the representative of the quackery Quaker church. Which of us shall prevail?" To the other man, he says, "Woodstock, take her in hand."

So, he *is* the father of Patience. Goodman Woodstock shoves me aside and stomps toward Pru, wrenching her away from Grace. "As God is my witness, I'll see you to Gallows Hill!" He yanks her arm until I think it could come free of the socket. Pity Patience with such a brute for a father.

I run to the door and flatten myself against it, though he's a head and shoulder taller than I and a hundredweight heavier.

Goodman Herrick pushes me aside with the back of his hand as if I'm a flitting fly. "Stand away, boy."

Woodstock marches Goody Pru out the door, and Constable Herrick pulls it closed, but not too quickly for me to notice Miss Patience jumping out of the way and her father shouting, "You do not belong here, daughter!"

Herrick growls, "Take your daughter home, Woodstock. I can manage this wretch on my own from here. There's room for her in the Salem jail—not far to go."

I close the door, and Grace and I fall into each other's arms.

"What shall we do, Thomas? Neither the God we know nor the God Goody Pru knows has saved her, and she won't survive a week in jail."

My thoughts as well. "Just rest, Grace. There, back to bed with thee. Thee must recover thy strength. Leave it to me to take care of our Pru."

But how?

Patience

"You put me to shame, daughter," Father barks, dragging me by the ear. "Did you see Goodman Herrick's daughter following him? No. A God-fearing daughter stays home where she belongs."

"Ahh, Father! You're twisting my ear. It'll come off in your hand."

He pinches harder. "I've a mind to see that your mother keeps you in the house. You've too much freedom to roam about during these dangerous times."

He grumbles and grouses all the way home until my head is swimming with his words and my ear is ringing as if a church bell were in my head. And all the while I'm wondering . . .

Did Thomas see me peeking around the corner of the house when the door flew open? If not, he surely noticed when Father led me away by the ear. How humiliating!

And of course he saw Father drag Goodwidow Blevins to Goodman Herrick's wagon, without a drop of gentleness.

And now Father tells me that *I've* put *him* to shame.

Repentance is in store again.

Chapter 19
June

Patience

Mother will not let me out of the house even for a minute. "I could use your help in the market. But your father insists, after your mucking about last night when he was on official village business, such as it was."

"But Mother . . ."

"Hush. Your father believes staying in the house alone will give you ample time to repent. Abigail will do her best with me and the fish."

"If she's not in one of her fits."

"No more will that happen, now that Sarah Good and Prudence Blevins are both behind bars."

"How long am *I* to be imprisoned?" I demand. There's not a breath of a breeze in this house. Even our candles are soft and bending. Human beings were not meant to survive where candles cannot hold up their own wicks. "What will I do all day, Mother, besides melt, and swat mosquitoes and gnats away?"

"Plenty. I shall leave you snap beans to trim and corn to shuck." She lays a basket of beans in my lap and a basket of corn beside my bench. Those scabby ears look unappetizing, though they're the ones rescued before pigeons and raccoons could chew the cobs bald and leave them good for nothing but kindling or privy fare.

"And yonder's a bushel basket of gooseberries begging to be tarts before they ferment. There's an eel swimming in that tub of water—won't live another day. Eel pie would be tasty for the noon meal. Get busy, Patience."

There's no end to the work of a woman. I glance at the eel, wriggling and black as night, and can't bear the thought of cooking him. I'll take my time, maybe all day, with the snap beans. The comforting rhythm of *snip, drop, ping* into the kettle sends me into a waking dream.

I'm called upon to repent my sins . . . but, to my shame, my sinful mind slides to Satan instead. I wonder what he actually looks like. Mercy Short describes him as a tall man of tawny hue, with straight black hair topped by a high-crowned black hat. Some people say it's a white hat, and others say he's not tall at all—that he's a three-foot-high, hairy, clawed animal. I would like to see for myself, but from a safe distance.

I wish I could hear from Mercy Short's lips about her own personal encounter with the Devil. What was she promised if she would go over to his side? I know what Betty Parris was promised—that she'd live in a great Golden City. Imagine such a place, the color of sunrise, gleaming and glittery.

Oh, but the other Mercy, Mercy Lewis, swears that Satan made himself look like Reverend George Burroughs and took her up to a very high mountain where she could see all the kingdoms of the earth. They could each and all be hers, he promised—not just Betty's Golden City—if only she'd write in his devilish book.

I wouldn't need all those kingdoms. Just one or two would do.

No! We are plain and simple people. I must not be tempted by such evil, empty promises. I shall remember the rest of what Mercy Lewis said: that if she refused to give her eternal soul to Satan, he vowed he'd tear her to pieces, break her neck, and throw her down the mountain.

The beans in my lap are done. My fingers barely remember touching them, and I have not repented yet. I suppose there is an excellent way to atone for my sins—whatever they are—by facing the slimy eel and rendering him into a spicy pie.

Thomas

Today the magistrates will examine Goody Pru to decide whether to set a trial date for her. I'm nearly first to arrive at the meetinghouse for the examination, but soon my friend Thatcher joins me.

"It's not a lesson day with Goodwife Willowby, is it, Thatch? No need to hide from your father?"

"No, but I hate to miss these wild circuses, and your own Goody Blevins is at the center of this one." He settles on the floor right in front of the magistrates' table. "Come sit by me. Best view from right here."

"First I'm presenting a petition to move this examination to a different location—perhaps Andover or Ipswich. Everyone here in Salem has already made up their minds about Goody Pru. She may get a fairer hearing elsewhere."

Thatch raises his eyebrows, his expression saying *hopeless, but good luck.*

I approach the magistrates' table, the petition fluttering in my shaky hand. Magistrate Hathorne quickly scans it, tosses it aside, looks up at me, and says, "You, the Quaker boy who will not sign an oath. That alone disqualifies you from submitting a petition such as this. No, we will not move Goodwidow Blevins's examination to a different venue. Stand aside."

Thatch was right. I had no chance of success. But I had to try.

Others flock in and sit or stand all around us, among them Abigail Woodstock and her mother. I'm disappointed that Miss Patience isn't with them. What's become of her since she watched the constables drag Pru from our house?

Pru shuffles in between two guards, each a foot taller than she is. Her hands are roped in front of her. She's tottering on her swollen feet, glaring at her neighbors who have come to see her accused. The judges launch familiar questions at her, but she's dead silent, not opening her mouth even to deny the charges.

Suddenly Abigail drops to the floor, yelling, "Ahhhhhh! The witch is jabbing me with long needles clear to my heart!"

Magistrate Hathorne pounds a gavel for silence. "Good denizens of Salem, I shall employ the Touch Test. Yeomen, untie the defendant's hands and lead her over to the afflicted girl."

Two men lift Abigail to her feet. She cowers with her head and shoulders thrust back and her hands raised for a shield.

The crowd goes silent. Hathorne's voice is the only one heard: "Defendant Prudence Blevins, by the authority of our sovereign king and queen, I order you to reach out and touch the afflicted child."

Pru defiantly slaps her hands to her sides until one of the yeomen raises her right arm and unfolds Pru's first finger. The knotted, wavery finger comes nearer until it rests on Abigail's shoulder. As suddenly as Abigail's fit began, it ends, and she sinks back against the men holding her up. Her mother rushes forward to steady her.

"Aha!" shouts Magistrate Hathorne. "Proof for all to witness: the witch has both caused the affliction and stopped it! Take her back to jail until she can be brought to trial later this month. Yeoman, bring in our next defendant."

I have to talk to Pru before they lock her away again. With Thatch at my side, I elbow my way through the crowd and outside. We reach Pru just as a yeoman is lifting her by her underarms and dropping her into a wagon as you would a sack of potatoes.

"May I have a word with her?" I plead.

"You can try. You won't get a sound out of her. Didn't know better, I'd say the witch swallowed her own tongue."

I lean low into the wagon and bend my head to Pru's ear. "Pru, listen, please. I'll do what I can to bring you home, but you must speak for yourself. Tell them that you're not in covenant with the Devil."

"What for, Thomas?"

The yeoman turns around to stare, surprised to hear her voice.

"Even if I say I'm no witch, they won't believe me, and I'll swing from a rope like Bridget Bishop and the others to come. Or I'll take my last breath in their Godforsaken jail, like Sarah Osborne. Just as dead either way." Pru's head jerks back as the wagon begins rolling.

I run after it to keep up. "I'll do what I can," I promise Pru again, but my words are drowned out by the *clop-clop* of the horse's hooves.

Thatch catches up to me as I stand watching the wagon lumber away. "Not true that she's just as dead either way," he says.

"Dead is dead, Thatcher."

"Think so? Did you hear what they're planning for Good-man Corey, on account of he won't say is he or is he not a witch? They'll lay the poor sot down on the ground and heap heavy weights on him, boulders and such, until every bone's crushed and every breath is snuffed out. Me, I'd rather hang. One, the rope's round your neck. Two, they pull the stool out from under you, and three, you drop. The end, quick and easy. That's how Sarah Good and them will go out, next week. Five of 'em, the nineteenth of July."

Chapter 20
July

Thomas

Mother used to say, *When things are at their worst, they begin to mend.* Things can't get much worse. Where's the mending?

At the cordwainer's, cleaning up with a rag does little good. The rag's as black as my hands and my blotched face, but I rub anyway while I think about things I've read in my law book.

Eventually I jag the silence between Goodman Cawley and myself. "Sir, may I speak to you?"

His giant needle pokes in and out of softened leather. "I don't like a lot of talk when I'm working, boy."

"I know that, sir, and I also know that you don't like to hear about the witchcraft business." No response; he doesn't even deign to look up. "But sir, I have no father to advise me, and you know everyone here in Salem."

"Not everyone. There's a man lives on Prospect Street I've not met."

From Goodman Cawley, this is humor!

"You've no doubt heard that Goodwidow Blevins is in jail, accused. Like you, sir, she has no son to speak up for her. It falls to me. What should I do?"

"Well, now, this I can help you with." He lays the swatch of leather on his lap and threads the tip of the needle through his shirt for safekeeping. "I heard Rebecca Nurse's family got up a petition about her case. More than thirty folk signed it, attesting to her good character. Almost got her freed. Almost, I say."

I can't think of even five people, much less thirty, who'd vouch for Pru. "Goodwife Nurse must be held in much higher regard than Goodwidow Blevins, sir."

"Well, then, turn it round: Talk to anyone who accuses the widow. See if they'll hold firm or not. The bewitched are generally young girls, I believe. Wouldn't be a terrible task to speak with them, now, would it?"

"Pleasant, almost," I agree. So far as I know, Abigail Woodstock is Pru's only accuser. To reach Abigail, I'll have to get past Miss Patience. "I know just where to start."

He slips the needle out of his shirt and takes up the leather again. "Too hot in here for two of us. What keeps you here? Be gone to your task, Thomas."

I believe Goodman Cawley must have been a decent father.

I lift my hat off the hook, snatch up my law book, and borrow a scrap of paper and a pencil for good measure. "Good day, Goodman Cawley. I'm off to the Woodstocks' house."

"Guard yourself, boy. Goodman Woodstock is a fiend and stinks of fish. I believe he eats the eyes and tails."

Patience
Sucking in the fresh air, I dash outside to help Abigail and Mother prepare the wagon for the morning trip to collect

Father's fish and bring them to the market. "How long am I to be an indentured servant in this house, Mother?"

"Until your father says."

"Most prisoners know when their sentence will end." Not little Dorothy, obviously, or Tituba or the other accused witches not yet brought to trial. But still, I stamp my foot, and my stockinged toe pokes out of the hole in my shoe. "Can't Abigail serve my sentence for me?"

"Thank you, good sister!" says Abigail tartly. "Haven't I suffered enough in this house?"

"You're perfectly fit and fine now. I don't believe you've been hauled off to the pasture the last few nights."

"None of that, daughters." Mother's glare puts an end to the argument but not to my petition.

"Mother, even the fish get to leave their homes!"

"And be clubbed to death in a goodwife's kitchen," she reminds me.

Abigail says, "Mother, I've so much more energy since that old witch got thrown in jail. Why don't you go in the wagon, and I'll walk to the market?"

"She's only doing that to taunt me, Mother, because I can go nowhere!"

After a deep sigh that probably means *Why did God give me such surly girls instead of a workhorse of a son?* she says, "Very well, Abigail. Patience, get that goose that's plumped up enough to be supper. You know the one I mean, Goodgoose Turnip. Give her neck a sound wringing and pluck her down to the pink. That'll give you plenty of fresh air."

There is no task I hate more.

"Go on, now, daughter, and be sure to collect every last feather. Turnip will be a fine new quilt, come winter." Mother climbs into the wagon. "Abigail, don't dally. I'll be needing your help right quick."

Mother drives off, and Abigail, of course, dallies. She's sitting on a log, writing those confusing alphabet letters in the soft dirt with a stick, when here comes someone weaving his way carefully along the lane through the ducks and chickens and hogs (and their droppings). By the look of disgust on his face, I can tell that Thomas Stillbrooke is not a lover of animals. Perhaps this is another Quaker characteristic. How dismal.

Thomas

"Come to sell me shoes, have you?" Miss Patience asks, and I notice that she hides the holey one behind her other heel. How long can she stand on one foot without falling over?

"No—in fact I've come to talk to your sister."

Miss Abigail jumps to her feet. "Me? Why?"

"It's about Goodwidow Prudence Blevins."

"I do not want to talk about that horrid witch," she says, then won't stop talking about her. "Once Sarah Good went off to jail and let me be, Prudence Blevins took over for her, doing the Devil's work right up until the time Father, God bless him, sent *her* off to jail."

I glance over at Miss Patience, who's on two feet now and hanging on every word. "Yes," I say, "your sister and I were both there when Goodwidow Blevins was stolen from her house."

"Stolen, bah! Captured like the dangerous wild creature she is. And don't call her a *good*widow. She's the wife of Satan, she is. She nearly tore me to pieces. Ripped out my gut. Wrenched my neck so hard I could barely turn it back-to-front. Dragged me out of my bed, still in my night shift, right through the window without it even opening, dragged me along the lane till my skin was flayed raw, out to the pasture behind good Reverend Parris's house. I was tormented near to death!"

I have to stop her or she'll go on through eternity. "Miss Abigail, you know that Goodwidow Blevins is old and of weak body. Her fingers are knotted, her feet the same. How was she able to do all this to you?"

"She's a witch, that's how!" Her words are ferocious, but her face says something different. I can't tell just what.

I want to ask her, *Could you have simply imagined all these horrors?* Or worse, *Could you be feigning the afflictions to bring attention upon yourself?*

Miss Patience says, "I can swear to the fact that the torments are real enough. We've prayed and fasted and had the doctor, and he believes her and wants to leech her."

My stomach turns upside down at the mere thought of leeches.

"You look poorly, Thomas, as though you'd gotten a sinewy piece of meat stuck in your throat," says Miss Patience. "Do your people even eat meat?"

"We do, when we have a shilling or two to spare, but that has nothing to do with why I'm here." I turn to Abigail. "Is it possible that Prudence Blevins herself isn't the one who did all these things to you?"

"She is!" Abigail shouts, and again I see something unexplainable flicker across her face.

"Perhaps it was the specter of Prudence Blevins, not the bodily person herself?"

"Well, I did see an exact copy of Prudence Blevins step right out of her. That what you mean?"

Ah, now we're getting somewhere. "So, is it possible that she didn't give the Devil permission to use her apparition? That Satan used her ill, and that she herself is innocent?"

"That's not one question, it's three," Abigail snaps. "I won't recant, if that's what you're asking. I won't take back a word I've said. And I'm needed at the market before Mother grows frantic."

Miss Patience sighs. "Thomas, I have a goose to pluck, so you'd best be on your way as well, or you'll have feathers in your hair and all over your fine clothes."

She's mocking my threadbare coat and breeches, even though she's tied a soiled apron over her plain muslin frock with its hem sweeping up yard dirt better than a broom could.

"And you, Miss Patience, are in your First Day finery, I see. I can still fix that hole in your left shoe."

Her face reddens. "No thank you." She waves her sister on down the road.

But before Abigail's ten steps away, she turns around. "The Touch Test," she calls across the distance between us.

"Yes?" I take paper and a pencil from my pocket, ready to write down what she says next.

"I was suffering so, and the judges made Prudence Blevins come over to touch me, to prove that she was the cause of it. It felt . . . different."

"Different how?"

Abigail picks up a goose and buries her face in its neck until it squawks and spreads its wings, wriggling out of her grip. "My torments stopped straightaway, but the touch—well, how to describe it? I'd felt that witch's evil hand many times, to be sure. But the warmth of *this* touch went right through my skin." She rubs her shoulder where Pru's finger tapped her that day. "It wasn't so much a *stop it* touch, which the magistrates ordered to prove her guilty, like when your fingers snuff out a candle." She demonstrates, tapping her thumb and first finger together. "It was more like a . . . like a . . . healing balm. It felt like someone else's touch entirely, not the witch's touch that I knew all too well."

Chapter 21
July

Thomas

"Sawtucket?" His head is tucked to his chest; he's either asleep or dead there on his rock. I tap his shoulder to be sure. "Sir?"

He slowly lifts his head. "Had me quite a dream. A plump goose, all crisped and greasy, just waitin' for me to sink me teeth into 'er."

My own stomach growls at the description. Grace and I haven't had a bite of juicy roast goose since before we left London. And there are plump ones in the Woodstocks' garden . . .

Stretching from his nap, Sawtucket's arms reach out like wings and fold back to his sides, though his palm turns out. Habit for a beggar, I suppose.

"Dark days for ye, lad. Heard Goody Blevins was trundled off to jail."

"How do you know about it if you never leave this rock that's worn down to cradle the shape of your hind end?"

He chuckles and pats his bony hip. "I'm paid to know things. It's me perfession. Suppose ye pity her, do ye?"

"She's not the gentlest soul, to be sure, but I hate the

thought of her being in jail." What comes to mind is Miss Patience's description of Dorothy lying in filth. "People have died from fever and pestilence, waiting for their trials." And yet, if she's done to Miss Abigail what the girl claimed, surely she *should* be punished. My head aches with the effort to sort it all out.

Sawtucket shrugs. "Most would say she deserves it, for covenantin' with the Devil, signin' his book. Should think I'd want to see that for meself, 'fore I make any moves."

The book. The meetings in the pasture. Has no one ever thought to go and see them? To catch the Satan-worshippers in the act and discover once and for all whose names are signed in blood in his book?

A dangerous plan takes shape in my head: attend a midnight witches' meeting, to see for myself the diabolical goings-on and whether Pru—or her specter—takes any part in them. The thought sends shivers down my back, even in this stifling heat.

With a grin, Sawtucket says, "Could be every bit as evil as what Goody Putnam swore about Goody Rebecca Nurse. Said that Goody Nurse threatened—her very words—to 'tear my soul out of my body.'"

"Not very helpful, Sawtucket."

"Nay, but don't it paint a pretty picture?"

Patience

A kettle of potatoes and carrots and tomatoes from our garden is stewing on the hearth for our noon meal, and Mother won't be home for an hour. What to do? Somehow my obstinacy draws me to the very thing that would make Father apoplectic. I sneak out of the house and over to the Salem jail to have a look at the woman Abigail calls a monster.

The air is stifling, and I breathe through my mouth to keep the stench out of my nose as the prisoners beg.

"Kind sister, can you spare me a bit of snuff? Tobacco?"

"Sugar?"

"A sturdy paper fan?"

"A thimbleful of whiskey?"

"A tumbler of cool, clean water?""

I have none of those, but still, for this jail visit I've come armed. That is, my arms are filled with carrots, and I thrust them into the hands extended through the bars. Each woman retreats to a corner like a dog to guard her treasure, and soon there's as much ferocious crunch-crunching as if we were in a rabbit warren. I've saved one carrot for Prudence Blevins.

Unlike the others, she's alone in her cell. She sits on the cot her jailers have issued her, with her own threadbare blanket round her shoulders, staring absently.

Slipping a small goose-down pillow out from under my cloak, I call softly, "Goodwidow Prudence, I've brought you gifts."

"Why?" the old woman barks.

I have no ready answer. When she doesn't come forward to accept what I'm offering, I stuff the pillow between the bars, and it drops to the dirt floor beside her. "Something to ease your back. Also, here's a carrot, fresh picked this morning." I extend it between the bars, but she doesn't reach for it. It drops and bounces off the pillow.

Goodwidow Blevins is shrunken, ancient. The hands nested in her lap are like twisted tree limbs. Her white hair wildly haloes her face, which is as wrinkled as a wrung-out rag. She looks harmless. And yet . . .

"Abigail Woodstock is my sister."

There's not a hint of recognition in her sunken eyes. "Two sisters I had, both rotted in their graves before you were born. Go away."

"Not yet, Goody. I've come to ask you a question about my sister, Abigail, who has suffered so."

"If you're asking did the Devil get into me, like all the rest of 'em ask me, you'll be rotting like *my* sisters before I'll say one way or the other."

Ingrate! Well, now I'm angry! "I beg your pardon," I say coldly. "It seems I'm wasting my time and yours." Squatting, I reach through the bars for the carrot, but as soon as I do I see her flinch. Her withered hand twitches as if to reach down and grasp the carrot, and she sucks in a hissing breath. And suddenly I realize: the woman's hungry and desperate and frightened out of her wits.

My heart gentles. Instead of snatching my offering back, I nudge it closer to her before withdrawing my hand. "The carrot is yours. And please rescue this pillow before it sops . . . whatever is on the floor. Rest well, and don't let the Devil whisper in your ear."

"Whisper? He shouts. Ah, get on with you, girl."

She's exasperating! But so am I, according to my mother. Evil is another matter altogether.

"I won't bother you any further today, Goodwidow Blevins, but I shall return another time if I can." I back away and dash through the corridor full of voices and outstretched hands.

The rabbits are done chawing, and I am out of carrots.

130

Thomas

I stop at the Cade family's carpentry tent, which smells nearly as fragrant as our shop, what with the clean particles of shaved wood carpeting the floor.

"Hallo, Thomas!" Thatch points to a table that gleams almost golden with high polish. "My latest," he boasts. "We don't just build scaffolds, you know."

"Fine work, Thatch. I've come to ask a favor. Will you help me save Goody Pru from the gallows?"

"Witch or not, you're fond of her, eh?"

"I believe she's innocent. I hope to find out, one way or the other."

Thatch nods. "I'd call that a righteous cause. How can I help?"

"You're good at slipping out of the house. Come with me to the witches' coven in Reverend Parris's pasture."

Thatch's eyes widen.

"I promise, this is not a Devil's proposition. I only aim to investigate what goes on out there."

Thatch blows air out of his puckered lips, flicks sawdust that's settled on his table, and grins broadly. "Just say when, my friend."

"Tonight, midnight."

Chapter 22
July

Patience

I've been freed! I don't dare ask Father what's ended my impris-
onment, but Mother says, "The worst of the danger's passed,
now that Prudence Blevins is to be brought to trial, and Sarah
Good is set to hang by the neck with those other four witches
tomorrow."

And Dorothy Good will be motherless.

"So, you shall come with me to fetch your father's morning
catch and tend the fish stall, Patience."

Even that sounds appealing after all the time I've spent in
this lonely house.

When we've readied the wagon, Mother hands me the
reins, which feels glorious after my confinement and consign-
ment to kitchen duty for so many days. I'm in no hurry, so I let
Molasses trot along at a slow clip until Mother says, "Step it up.
We're missing the early morning crowd."

We've not been tending our stall long when Goodman
William Good comes stumbling through the market square,
more drunk than usual.

Mother whispers, "Hasn't seen a sober day since his wife

was arrested." And since he testified against her.

Stopping in front of our baskets of cod and bass, he rests his hands on his knees and blinks a few times to clear his eyes. "Sorry to tell ye, Goody, but I fear that fish is plain dead."

All our fish are dead, save the last handful that Father caught this morning, which swim in a bucket of water. And they're not long for this world either.

"Turnin' putrid, by the look of it," William Good observes.

"I do not sell putrid fish," says Mother with disgust. "You are a drunken disgrace. Go sleep it off."

He comes out of his crouch and stands as tall as his rubbery legs will allow. "I'm drunk for good reason, ye know. Good reason."

I take this as an opportunity. "Goodman Good, I worry about your daughter, little Dorothy. Have you been to the Ipswich jail to see her? She's in sore need of care."

He gazes at me steadily through squinty eyes, as if he's lost what he meant to say.

"Hrumph," Mother mumbles. "Care, from this sodden sort?"

He ignores Mother's words, or else he's too drunk to hear them. "Would, but I don't have it in me. Me-o-my-o, poor William. Wife's a witch, daughter's a witch, and the other one a jailbird." He must mean the baby that's been growing inside Sarah Good.

Mother says, "Born, the pitiful waif was?"

Goodman William tilts his head as if listening for an answer from the sunshine. His eyes light up and quickly dim. "That one, name of Mercy, dead afore she opened her eyes. So my witch wife had no chance to put the Devil in her."

Mother hands him a small fish, good for two bites once cooked. Quietly, she says, "Go home, William."

"I've got no home, Goody Woodstock. No woman, no little ones, and in the morning—that would be tomorrow, or was it yesterday?—whichever—my poor wife will hang." He swings his first finger back and forth like a pendulum.

Thomas

"Never been to a witches' meeting," says Thatcher, full of false bravado. Like me, he carries a fat candle, its flame fluttering in the midnight breeze. Several of the confessed witches say they've flown over the tops of trees to these gatherings. I sincerely doubt this, but anyway Thatcher and I have no such transport, so we trudge along in the hot, humid dark.

"How do they know when to gather?" Thatch asks. "Or do they meet every night, same time, same place?"

"I know no more than you," I tell him. "Though remember, some of the accused have spoken of a pipe or a trumpet call summoning them. Think of it as a siren song luring us to danger, like in Homer's *Odyssey*."

"Who's Homer, one of your Quaker friends?"

Startled, I realize that Thatcher's father isn't the kind who'd read this epic poem aloud to his children, as Father did for Grace and me. "No, an ancient Greek poet. Never mind. Just hush and keep walking."

We never hear a trumpet, but we are not alone for long.

Others in dark clothes silently slip out of their houses and make their way toward the edge of the village. By the time we pass the parsonage and reach the vast field stretching out behind it, there's quite a flock of us, maybe fifty souls. Faces are lit by the glow of candles and of torches made from pine tree splints. Frenzied whispers blend with a riot of cicada song.

I search faces for the spectral image of Pru, if such a thing exists. If I see her here, I must determine whether she willingly gave her soul to Satan for this apparition or if the Devil snatched her innocent soul without her permission. I could easily miss spotting her specter, with this crowd whirring in constant motion in the dark. Thatch, the one who's boldly planted himself in the front row at every witch's examination and trial, now hangs back, but I want to see and hear what's going on, so I drag him by the arm toward the front of the throng.

A steady thrumming seems to synchronize all our heartbeats. Near me is a girl about my age, her face aglow in the candlelight. My curiosity defeats my shyness. "May I ask what brings you here tonight?"

"Promises," she murmurs. "We need only sign his book, and all will be ours."

"What are you promised?"

She raises her candle toward my face and smiles. "Something better, something freer, richer, I know not what yet." She swishes her skirt and curtseys. "Maybe I shall have a gown of fine crimson silk and French lace. And golden trinkets for my hair."

Such small, simple rewards. A bit of finery. A bit of freedom.

"This is not the only world, you know." She whips off her bonnet and throws it to the wind, allowing a waterfall of dark hair to flow down her back. I feel the current of that fall and long to step into it.

This is temptation! The Devil's handiwork!

I've all but forgotten that Thatcher is beside me when his familiar voice carries under the buzz of so many murmurings.

"Too much, Thomas. Let's go home." He can't see me shake my head, but he stays, his shoulder pressed to mine. The air around us is charged with energy as if before a fearsome storm. I tilt my head back to watch for electric slashes in the black sky. The night fairly throbs with . . . what? With anticipation.

A small man of some forty years climbs onto a tree stump in front of us. He is all in black: his clothes, his hair, the high hat crowning his head. It's just as the accused witches have testified. My heart quickens, my stomach knots. Am I witnessing the Devil incarnate? I stagger with the possibility. Thatch steadies me.

"Who's that man?" I ask Thatch, but he seems not to hear me. His glowing eyes, lit by his candle, look almost demonic, and for a moment I wonder if *he's* a witch, a wizard, drawn into the Devil's snare. Maybe he's only frightened, as I am, in the awesomely powerful forces around us.

I lean toward the girl beside me and whisper in her ear. "Could you kindly tell me, who is that man up there?"

She gapes at me in astonishment. "You don't know? That's George Burroughs. Once he was the minister here, when I was a small child." Her sudden smile is triumphant. "Satan covets ministers, and, oh, how they thrash about when he draws them over to our side! Now he's the leader of us all."

I shake my head—to convince myself? Surely this cannot be George Burroughs because he's locked up in the Boston jail, awaiting his trial as a witch. He simply cannot be *there* and *here* at the same moment.

The crowd grows silent, except for the breathing of half-a-hundred souls in high expectation. As if at a signal from the stars above us, we one by one snuff out our candles, our torches. We're left in daunting darkness.

Finally, the man speaks. His voice, though soft, carries as if he were shouting: "Who among us is free of sin?"

My shoulders sag in relief, or is it disappointment? He isn't the Devil. Why, he's just another Puritan preacher giving a sermon.

"Your sins, as your neighbors call them, are natural. They are what separate us from beasts of burden. You have every right to a bit of comfort, a bit of pleasure—every right to command the course of your own lives! Why bow and scrape before those who call themselves representatives of God, when you could stand upright and serve the one who asks only that you follow your instincts? Follow the one who accepts you as you are, not as you pretend to be. You are not alone. You need not live in shame. Join him, and find your true home."

We step back a pace or two to make way for several black-cloaked, hooded men. Theirs are the only candle flames dancing and sputtering in the dark. They scurry about and slide in and out of one another's shadows, hiding from my view the man who is *not* the Devil. The crowd packs around me, surging forward, with outstretched arms. I unwittingly reach too, though I don't know what I'm reaching for. Is Thatcher still beside me? I can't tell.

Suddenly, the sea of shadowy figures parts. There's a collective gasp. The man is . . . gone. In his place, on the tree stump, sits a small creature, its amber eyes glowing in the light of a torch.

"What happened?" I ask the girl next to me, struggling to make sense of what I'm seeing and not seeing.

"Did you not see for yourself? He's transformed into his familiar, Goodman Burroughs has!"

Preposterous. Sleight-of-hand, of course, in the impenetrable dark, but the crowd pressing in around me is ardently convinced that the one they believe to be George Burroughs has changed into a diabolical gray cat.

Patience

Suddenly I awaken and bolt upright in the stifling loft. Something is wrong. I have this gnawing feeling in my heart that someone I care about is in trouble.

Abigail, for once, is sleeping peacefully beside me. I climb down the loft ladder and peek at Mother and Father's bed. Father's snoring and Mother's face is sunk into her pillow, but I see her back move with her breathing.

I think I hear faint distant music—the Baptists or the Catholics, maybe—but it could just be my own heart singing mournfully. I unlatch the window. Leaning out of it, I crane to see behind the house, toward the shack where the Goods used to lay their heads.

And now I know why I've awakened with such dread in my heart. Tomorrow, the nineteenth of July, at sunup, five women will be led to the gallows, and Goodwife Sarah Good will be among them.

My poor Dorothy.

Chapter 23
July

Thomas

The gray cat slinks down off the tree stump. Before it's lost in the crowd, its muscular tail winds around my leg. Shivers run up and down my spine and I'm left shaking like a sail in a storm. They say we are called Quakers because our bodies quake when we're touched by the Holy Spirit within us.

This is not a *holy* spirit.

"I want out," Thatcher says, backing into the crowd. "You coming, before it's too late to get away?"

I can't speak, just wave him off with a trembling hand. I should feel lost and alone without Thatch, but others meld into the space he's left. I'm swept into the energies around me. Power, light, the pungent scent of melting tallow candles. And now a low chanting has begun like the buzzing drone of a swarm of bees: *We serve you serve us we serve you serve us we serve you serve us.*

It's nearly impossible to resist falling into the chant that fills the air all around me. I clap my hand to my lips but taste the sacrilegious words in my palm. I will not give voice to them. I will not give in to them.

On the tree stump where the cat sat a moment ago, a great book is laid open. A man's commanding whisper slices through the din to ride above the wave of others' voices.

"Come, come, do not be afraid. Step forward. Sign the book, and unimagined rewards shall befall you. Dip this quill into my horn of red ink, thick and warm and rich as blood."

His words are soothing as a mother's lullaby, yet stirring at the same time. I'm swept forward with the throng, which is a tidal wave I cannot fight. In my heart of hearts, I *know* that a good soul—and I was born a good soul—cannot be possessed by Satan. And yet . . .

I'm borne forward by the crowd until I'm only a few hand-spans away from the book. There I see dozens of jagged blood-red marks. Each must be a soul Satan has claimed as his own. My eyes are bleary. I cannot read any names.

"Come, lad, sign," says the hypnotic voice. The crowd pushes against my back, my shoulders, my arms, so crushed in against me that I can barely breathe. I look up at the people clustered around me like a family, urging me to commit myself. To join them, to be welcomed by them—I who have no mother, no father.

I lift my eyes Heavenward to the distant twinkles of light. The moon is hidden. Hiding its face in shame? And there is Father, in the canopy of black sky, fathoms deep, and still his words reach into my mind:

Thee is a son of God, Thomas, a keeper of the Inner Light. Through God's grace, thee has free will.

This is not the only world, you know, said the girl with the beautiful hair.

A feather quill slides into my hand. I hold the quill a finger-length above the horn of red ink.

Thy mother and I implore thee, think. THINK, as we have taught thee, before thee chooses thy fate.

I'm suddenly racked with thirst, so parched I could drink the ink.

No! A force within me silently shouts the word.

I drop the quill into the pot of blood, thrust myself backward through the crowd, and stumble across the pasture, back toward the lane. My breathing is ragged, but now I'm free from the clutches of Satan, who was borne on the shoulders of all those deluded dreamers.

Safe. Saved.

Suddenly a rope loops around my neck.

I clutch at it, but it only grows tighter as my captor jerks me toward him. Constable Herrick.

"You will come with me to Salem jail, you agent of the underworld arts. A sinner you are, Quaker boy, a bewitcher cavorting with the Devil. You'll hang like the rest of 'em."

Patience

This is the first morning in my whole life that Father hasn't gone for the fish. Even on his wedding day; even on the days Mother gave birth to Abigail and me; even on days when fever raged in his body or storms loomed on the horizon, he was out on the water before dawn to chase the fish.

Today, he's sleeping, and it's well past dawn. Mother's wringing her hands in a fret. "I cannot rouse him! He wakes and turns his head back to his pillow. Has the Devil got him? What to do, what to do?"

Abigail and I try to stir him. "Father? Are you ill? Shall we pray together? Say the Lord's Prayer forward and backward? Call for a doctor?"

He opens one eye, looks out the window to see the sky. "Not yet." The eye slides shut.

Just as sunlight begins to slither under the door into our house, along with a refreshing morning breeze from the western window, Father rises from the bed, running his hands over the bristles on his chin. "Today, Bethia and my lovely daughters . . ."

When has he ever called us lovely?

". . . today is a grand day in Salem. Today we rid ourselves of the scourge of five witches. Come with me to Gallows Hill." He tightens his belt and rolls down his sleeves, bends to lace his Lord's Day boots, and throws the door open on a bath of sunlight. "Come, come."

"No, I will not," Mother says, dropping onto the bench.

Her shocking defiance emboldens me. "Nor I, Father. I can't bear to watch our townsmen hang Dorothy's mother and the other four, witches or not. You can't either, can you, Abigail?"

A dark cloud covers Abigail's face as she looks from me to Father. My heart aches for my sister. She is torn in so many directions.

She squares her shoulders. "None of you know how I've suffered at the hands of Sarah Good and her lot. I will go with Father to Gallows Hill."

Smiling proudly, Father tips his hat to Mother as he and Abigail step into the new morning sun.

How is it possible that the horror of a public hanging could happen on such a beautiful blue-sky day as today?

Thomas

The break of dawn is the last light I see before I'm tossed onto the dirt floor of a crowded cell that runs with God knows what fluids. The stench is overwhelming. The men descend upon me looking for food, tobacco, whiskey, snuff, anything they can use or trade for something better. One rips off my boots and jams his own bare feet into them. Another dents my hat as a pillow on the floor. When they're content that there's nothing left on me to comfort them, they leave me to my useless self and my sorry reflections.

Father, I heeded thy words. I resisted temptation, and yet here I lie among drunks and thieves and accused witches. Thee has let me down, Father.

In the next moment, I rethink it: *No, I have let myself down, allowing the better part of me to be drawn nearly into the Devil's net of soulless evil.*

How easily it could happen. The innocent and guilty alike become enthralled in the surging host of faithful *believers*, in their chants, in the candlelight, in the tempting voice whispering in their ears. Even the stars above seem to wink their approval of the demonic sacraments. After all, those gathered ask for so little: a few shillings, satins and trinkets, a seat at a sumptuous table. A few strands of silky hair.

Here in this dark, starless place, the reeking man nearest me kicks the heels of my boots on the only dry corner of the cell, raising a dust that adds to my thirst. His rusty words are slurred by last night's drink. "Me, I'm a fool and a sot," he says. "How about you, boy?"

"You a witch?" asks the man curled at our feet. "This jail's full of 'em."

"I am not a witch."

He scoffs. "That's what they all say."

I argue no further. I think of the accused people brought before the magistrates and judges—some seemingly guilty, others seemingly innocent. I think of George Burroughs, the accused ringleader, who was supposedly with us last night. Did his specter truly appear? Or did our fevered minds impress his image upon another man's face? Either way, if a minister can be arrested for witchcraft, surely no one is above suspicion.

And I *was* tempted. Just as these hapless drunks were doubtless tempted by the thought of one more tankard of rum, one more drink to dull their worries and their regrets.

But aren't they, aren't all of us, worthy of God's grace? A line from the Prophet Micah that Father often quoted comes to mind: *You will again have compassion on us; you will tread our sins underfoot and hurl all our iniquities into the depths of the sea.*

A soothing thought. But the Prophet Micah does not preside over Salem's courts of law. What's to become of me now?

✳

Time passes. How much time, I don't know. This cell grows so dark that I can only sense my cellmates by their stirring that causes the hot, humid air to move slightly. Father begged me to think, and that is what I do now, even as my stomach hollows into a ferocious hunger and my throat chafes, parched as dust.

Think. *Think.* Someone must tell Grace what's happened to me. Not that she can help me. Who *can* help me? Goody Pru herself is locked up. Maybe Thatcher, if I had a way to reach him. Patience Woodstock, perhaps? No, her father would never allow it.

There is only one person I can turn to—Goodman Cawley. But there's no way to get a message out of this dungeon. I have nothing to bribe a guard with.

The men around me stir as we hear the rumble of wagon wheels on the street above us. More than one wagon, it seems.

The man who uses my hat for a pillow pokes me. "On their way to Gallows Hill with the five of 'em. Sit up, mate, pay yer respects."

Chapter 24
July

Patience

After Sarah Good's hanging, Father brings the whole dreadful scene home to us.

"She was stubborn to the end. The good reverend—not Reverend Parris, but Reverend Noyes from the Salem Town congregation—well, he begged her to confess to her witchcraft, to put her soul at ease. She wouldn't. She spat the reverend's words back at him, called him a liar. Imagine the gall of the woman, talking to a man of the cloth that way! She'll surely burn in hell."

My heart skips a few beats. "What if she was telling the truth?"

"Truth, indeed!" scoffs Mother, before Father can do worse than scold me. "I wonder about you, Patience. Did you come from my body, or did someone drop you on our doorstep swaddled in rags?"

There are times I wonder as well. Why do I constantly wonder about everything?

I glance at my sister. Her face is the color of bleached muslin. Her trembling hands nested in the folds of her skirt tell me that she's trying to blot the images of the hanging from her mind. I certainly would be, in her shoes. I ask nothing of her just now.

Wondering again . . . Has anyone told Dorothy that her mother has gone to meet her fate in the next world?

Father says, "Five swinging from the gallows, but we're not yet finished with witches. Constable Herrick told me he caught the troublemaker boy, that haughty Quaker one, roaming by Reverend Parris's pasture last night. He's locked up now. Good riddance."

They have Thomas Stillbrooke in custody? My heart leaps to my throat. "Why? What has he done, Father?"

"Like the others of his kind, he's guilty of witchcraft."

This I will not believe. He's no more a witch than little Dorothy is. "No! Not Thomas. He's not like the other Quakers." Before the words are even out of my mouth, I'm questioning them. That gentle boy who refuses to strike another human being—is he indeed an exception among his brethren, the only one worthy of regard? If God's word to us in our meetinghouse is the same as His word to Thomas's people in theirs, who are we to say there is no goodness, nothing to admire in the whole lot of them?

But I must set these musings aside, for Mother is giving me a warning look. "What do you know of this Thomas Stillbrooke, daughter?"

I'd best be careful. "I met him a time or two when he was looking for customers for his master, Goodman Cawley the cordwainer." I cannot abide the thought of Thomas wallowing in a filthy cell. And all because he was walking near Reverend Parris's pasture at night?

But I dare not say more in front of Father. I wait until Mother and I are on our way to the market the next morning.

"No one has accused Thomas Stillbrooke of doing harm to others," I tell her. "Surely it's a mistake for him to be in jail. We must get him out!"

"Why would it fall to us, Patience? We're not his kin, and he's not one of our flock. He's someone else's problem."

I swallow the words bubbling to the surface, but poor Molasses gets the worst of my suppressed feelings when the whip comes down a bit heavier on her.

Thomas Stillbrooke would not strike a horse in frustration.

In the back of the wagon, the baskets of father's latest catch jostle, and water sloshes from the one precious bucket of still-living fish as Molasses trots on toward the market square, obedient despite my unkindness.

"And I suppose poor Dorothy Good is someone else's problem as well?" I ask at length.

Mother huffs. "She has a father, still."

"He's no fit caretaker for her! You're the first to say so. He'll let her hang for witchcraft, as he let her mother hang."

A shudder passes through Mother, though she tries to hide it. "If the town fathers thought it fitting to hang Dorothy, they'd have done it by now."

"Instead they've left her to rot in that dreadful jail. There must be a way to free her."

"And then do what with her?"

"Bring her home."

Mother's laugh flies to the wind. "There is not one jot of a chance. Not now that she's a confessed witch. Your father would faint dead away."

Hope rises in my heart as Molasses slows near the square. "Are you saying *you* would welcome Dorothy, but Father would forbid it?"

"Did I say that?" Mother asks crossly. She spits seeds over the side of the wagon, so many that I suspect a boysenberry bush will sprout there, come spring.

Thomas

Days have passed. How many? Enough for four bowls of thin gruel and a cup of brackish water, which I ration but crave in this airless cell. We're down to three of us. The two drunks sobered up and were released. That leaves the man who uses my hat as a pillow and the one who's wearing my boots, which I eye enviously as the dirt of the floor grinds between my toes.

I hear some sort of disturbance coming from the top of the long flight of stone stairs. A girl's voice.

"No, sir, I will not go to the women's section! I am here to see my brother, and you will not stop me." Ah, it's Grace!

I hear some rustling, some heavy breathing, and her shout: "Let go of me! I see that you're no gentleman. Now, kindly hand me your lantern, sir." There's more tussling, and I imagine her wresting the lantern away from the guard. She's ferocious, my sister!

Now comes the pounding of her shoes as she runs down the illuminated stairs. I see her, clutching something to her bodice—a lump wrapped in cloth. "Thomas? Thomas Stillbrooke!"

Other prisoners thrust their hands out at Grace, and some of the men whistle at her and call out, "Dolly, gimme-gimme-gimme, pretty wench."

"Do you gentlemen not have mothers and sisters?" Grace asks. "If one of them were to come here, would you want your friends to be so churlish? Thomas, where are thee?"

"Here, Grace." I wave between the bars, and she grabs my hand.

"Oh, Thomas! I've been beside myself with worry, alone in that house. I looked everywhere, asked everyone, even Sawtucket. Three times I went to Goodman Cawley's shop, and he knew nothing except that thee hadn't come to work. He was none too pleasant about it. How does thee tolerate that grumbler?"

I open my mouth to answer, but she's not through.

"The last time I was in his shop thy friend Thatcher stopped by, and he told me where thee had been the night before the hanging. Why on earth, Thomas? Why would thee go to such a gathering?"

"To find out what I could about Pru—whether she was there, in form or in spirit."

Grace makes an impatient noise. "And?"

"I never saw her."

"Well, I went to that man Corwin to inquire, and he told me thee'd been arrested. Lord almighty, *arrested*! Oh, thee must be so hungry."

Drawn by that word, my cellmates rush to the bars. From the cloth-wrapped package she carries, Grace hands me a heel of dark bread.

I gnaw off a chunk too large to chew before I tear the rest in half for my cellmates. While they're busy devouring the royal meal, Grace slips an apple into my pocket. She offers me a small flask of ale, and I drink the whole thing down, feeling guilty about my thirsty mates.

"Thee must get me out of here, Grace."

She sniffs the air. "Yes, it's revolting. But Corwin says thee must be practicing witchcraft, because thee was found near

Reverend Parris's pasture in the dead of night, the place and time when the witches are known to meet. What shall I do?"

"Go back to Goodman Cawley. He knows everyone in Salem Village." Except that man on Prospect Street. "He'll know who to call upon before they drag me to an examination and demand that I confess."

"What if he won't come, Thomas?"

A distinct possibility. "If Goodman Cawley will not come, go to Goodman Murdock at the shipyard. But try Cawley first." I swallow the rest of my bread and feel it thud to my empty stomach. Leaning close to Grace's ear, I whisper, "Tell Goodman Cawley that someone stole my boots." I jerk my head toward one of the cellmates. "Tell him I need new boots *right away*."

She nods. "Yes, yes, that will bring him. And I can be very persuasive."

"I know that better than anyone. My sister, the tiger. Now go to Cawley." I can't tolerate another night of sweat here, with my face in the dirt.

A guard appears. "Come, miss. Can't leave ye here among the rabble." He reaches for her, but she jerks her arm away.

"I shall walk on my own, thank you. Would you kindly hold the lantern to guide a lady's steps?"

A tiger, but always polite. Mother would be so pleased.

I count the minutes, listening for footsteps in the jail or horses' hooves out on the ground above us. After hours and another deposit in the overflowing slop bucket, a bowl of runny gruel arrives, this time without a spoon. I pick out the fleas and stash the gruel away for later. Perhaps Goodman Cawley will come before I must lap it up like a dog or slurp it off my filthy fingers.

Chapter 25
July

Thomas

Time slogs by. I can't tell if it's night or day, or how many days have passed in this dungeon. When my spirit is at its lowest and I feel forsaken by everyone, even God, Goodman Cawley finally comes.

He has me out of my cell before I know what's happened. "You're free and clear, boy."

I'm so relieved that I grab Goodman Cawley by his collar, though my grubby fingers let go quickly. "Thank you, sir! I know the world is full of wonders, but how did you manage this miracle?"

"Had a word with Corwin. Explained that I sent you on an errand, the night of the eighteenth, that took you near the pasture. Pure chance that you happened to be there when Constable Herrick was out on the prowl."

"And Corwin took your word for that?" My voice betrays my disbelief.

"My mother was a Phips," he says simply.

"You mean, you're related to our new governor, Sir William Phips?"

Goodman Cawley casts up his eyes in disdain. "I don't

think much of the connection, myself. Helps, though, from time to time."

"I'm grateful, Goodman Cawley. I wouldn't have survived another night steaming like an oyster in that cell with the fleas and rats." Just thinking of the vermin makes my skin crawl, and I scratch my arm until little beads of blood pop out.

"Christian thing to do, that's all. Your sister's made quite a nuisance of herself, hotheaded badgerer that she is. And I've heard that three men died of jail fever before they could come to trial. I caught you as an apprentice; I'm not letting you off the hook one day short of seven years."

"I'll be here for all of it."

"Well, don't stand there woolgathering. There's boots and shoes to be nailed and sewn up. You can't leave an old man to do it all, can you, now?"

Back at the shop, I fetch a half-made boot and mold the soft leather draped over the toe.

"I'm recalling you write pretty," Goodman Cawley says while we work. "You're to write me up a paper, legal and proper."

"Now, Goodman Cawley?"

"Naw, not now. I'm still thinking on it. I'll let you know when I'm set." He lowers his spectacles to the tip of his nose and meets my eyes. "After the Blevins trial. Comes up on Friday, did you know? I expect I'll shut the shop that day and go to Boston or Andover. Anywhere but here."

*

"Sawtucket, sir, I don't know who else to ask . . ."

He yanks his tattered topcoat down to look respectable. "I'm yer man. What's on yer mind, lad?"

"It's about Goodwidow Blevins. I believe she's innocent, but what good does my belief do her? Abigail Woodstock won't recant her accusation."

"Ye're askin' what to do?" His hand comes up, palm flattened, and I put a coin on it that disappears into his pocket. "I saw ye carryin' that book what could crack a head if it fell off the shelf. Ye're a lawyer-type. Make a case."

"I got nowhere when I asked for the examination to be moved. Or when I spoke to Magistrate Corwin about Dorothy Good, for that matter."

"Not the point, boy. Point is, make a case for Goody Blevins at her trial."

"You mean a solid defense? With evidence and witnesses and statements and all that?"

"What'd I just say, lad? Ye're clever enough not to need me to tell ye a third time."

Make a case. I haven't much to go on. But it's the only chance I've got to keep Prudence Blevins alive until she's called to her natural death, when her fate will be up to God.

Chapter 26
July

Thomas

It takes every bit of my courage and a cast-iron stomach to return to the jail. This time I venture into the women's section, late at night when most of the prisoners are sleeping and I can speak quietly to Pru. I'll only get a few minutes with her, so I'll not put up with any of her nonsense.

"Goody Pru, speak or not, but listen to me, please. This Friday you will be on trial before the court. If they convict you, you will hang. Do you understand what I'm telling you?"

I'm not sure she's listening, or if she can even hear me. She's huddled on a cot, with her thin blanket swaddling and her head on a grimy pillow that some kind soul must've left her. And she's shaking with fever.

"Whether you want to live or not, I'll aim to persuade the judges to spare your life."

Weakly, she says, "What makes you, a lowly cordwainer's apprentice, clever enough to hold his own before all those rich learned men at a witch trial? Answer me that, Thomas."

"I've been studying a law book from Harvard College. At your trial I'll show the judges where it says in the book that you're entitled to a defense. I'll speak up for you."

Pru struggles into a sitting position, the blanket hooded around her head and clasped to her chin. "Why are you doing this? I'm not your mother, nor kin of any kind."

"You've given Grace and me a roof over our heads and shared what little you had, even though we are not of your faith. We're in your debt."

"That you are. But I'm beyond your help now, Thomas. I shall die in this Godforsaken place."

"No. Listen to what I say." I can't waste words, even if I sound disrespectful. "Here's what you must do at the trial on Friday." If she lives that long. "First, give up the absurdity of neither confessing nor denying that you're a witch. This stubbornness may seem like a virtue, but it accomplishes nothing for your body or your soul. Next, answer the judges' questions clearly and honestly. You must appear as a reasonable, Gospel-loving, unblemished soul."

"I'm not. Would I be suffering so if I were without sin?"

"You and I think differently about sin, Pru. You believe that illness and misfortune are punishments for sin. I don't, but this is no time for a religious debate. Do you know the words to the Lord's Prayer?"

"Been saying it every day of my life."

"Good. Now, as far as I can tell, Abigail Woodstock is the only one accusing you, and she truly has been afflicted. So here is a most important question: Do you believe that Satan used your image to torment Abigail Woodstock?"

"That Father of Lies, that Old Serpent, the Master Deluder."

"And did you give the Devil the use of your image of your own free will?"

"Not on your life or immortal soul, Thomas."

I hear the guard's footsteps. "Then pray, Pru. Pray for God to strengthen you, to lift all curses from you, to heal you so you can come to the trial and hear the judges say the words *not guilty*. Then Grace and I shall take you home."

"No herbs nor potions in this Godforsaken dungeon, but a spot of tea would help with the healing."

"I'm sorry, I have none." Nor do I have much confidence in the potions and elixirs that Goody Pru touts, but I *am* a believer in the curative power of faith, of which she has plenty.

"Well! If you're set on speaking up to those judges, then you ought to be able to convince the jailer to bring me a cup of tea. I'll not hold it against you if there's no sugar in it, nor milk to whiten it." She already sounds stronger, almost her old feisty self.

Patience

"No! I will not go to the trial with you." Abigail stamps her foot and wraps her arms around herself protectively while Mother argues with Goodwife Simms over the price of a sturgeon huge enough to feed her family of eight.

"But you're her accuser!" I say, as if Abigail needs reminding. "You're expected to testify."

"All she has to do is come near, and I'm in torment," Abigail says. "I will not let that woman hurt me ever again."

"Then I'll go without you." I resist the urge to stamp my foot like Abigail did, though it's frightening to think of being at the trial alone today. Well, I'm very good at tangling fear into a web of righteous anger, but where to put that anger?

I settle on Goodwife Simms. "Goody, a beautiful sturgeon

like this one, caught not two hours ago? Why, it's a prize beyond words, worth whatever Mother asks, wouldn't you agree?"

Mother flashes me a look of surprise, but Goody Simms pays full price and walks away with the flopping fish she needs both arms to carry.

I hop on the advantage I've just gained. "Mother, I feel a duty to go to Goody Blevins's trial, for Abigail's sake."

"Yes, yes, see that your sister gets justice for her suffering," Mother says. "God willing, this will be the end of it all." Her voice reaches for its usual briskness but falls short. Is it the glinting sun, or do I see tears in her eyes? I haven't seen her shed a tear since Father's boat was caught in a sudden thunderstorm last summer and he didn't return to shore for twelve agonizing hours.

Now she turns to the two goodwives who've stepped up to our stall with coins jangling.

In the road, geese and chickens avoid the hogs. I need to step around the animals and their leavings to get to the meetinghouse, which is already filling with our curious and vengeful neighbors. Truth be told, I've been hoping that Thomas Stillbrooke would be among them, and he is, but my heart hammers my throat when I see him come in with . . . a girl!

Thomas

I lead Grace over to a post we can lean against while the judges hear the four cases ahead of Goody Pru's. To my surprise, my master, Goodman Cawley, is working his way through the crowd to stand with us. Didn't he say he'd be in Boston today? He doffs his hat to Grace and gives me a quick nod. I'm grateful to have him at my side, especially when I see the men around us defer to him. They must know his mother was a Phips.

And there is Miss Patience, coming in alone. How odd that her sister isn't with her to bear witness against Pru. Perhaps that will work in our favor. Or perhaps it will merely be seen as proof of Miss Abigail's tormented state.

The morning rushes by, with me listening to every word I might use. Grace looks more and more stricken as, one by one, four of the accused are convicted, sentenced to hang, and sent back to jail.

By the time the judges and jurors get to Goody Pru, they seem weary, or perhaps bored—or possibly I've misread them and they're girded for battle. Unlike the other defendants, who stumbled in with their hands bound, Pru is carried on a stool by two guards and placed in front of the judges' table. Her hands are free. Grace and I step forward, Grace to see to Pru's comfort and me to plead her case.

I catch Pru's eye, hoping she'll read the message I'm sending: *Do not confess, no matter how much pressure they put on you. Be reasonable in your answers. And, for God's sake, be good.*

"Grace, stay here while I talk to the magistrates." She reluctantly lets go of my arm. I can see that she's uneasy; this is her first time attending a public trial.

When I was Grace's age, thirteen, Father took me to Old Bailey for the trial of a man who'd stolen tools from the shipyard where Father worked. He explained to me about the plaintiff who accused the defendant of the theft, the defendant who had to disprove the evidence against him, the judge, and the jury. But there was no one in that London courtroom doing what I intend to do for Goody Pru—no one defending the defendant.

Gathering my courage, I nod to the jury and approach the

judges' table—three judges today, as I suppose they cannot all be present for every trial when they must attend to other pressing matters.

"Magistrate Hathorne, Magistrate Corwin, and—I'm sorry, but I do not know the third judge's name."

"Stoughton," he says. "Chief justice." He gazes at me steadily but not with hostility. I take strength from that.

"Sirs, I am representing Goodwidow Prudence Blevins today."

Hathorne and Corwin exchange amused looks. Corwin says, "This is not customary in an English common law court. Enough of your frivolities, boy."

"It is no frivolity, sirs. I will speak for Goodwidow Blevins, as I have been studying the law—modestly, I must add—and I've learned that the accused is entitled to a defense."

"What do you expect to accomplish, boy?" demands Corwin. "Do you expect that your audacity will make your parents proud?" I suspect he's implying the opposite, or maybe he's heartlessly reminding me that I'm an orphan.

I try to look humble, recalling how Father often quoted Proverbs: *Pride goeth before destruction, and a haughty spirit before a fall.* I must not fall. "Sirs, I've no aim except to help this court find the truth."

"Stand back," Hathorne says sternly, but Chief Justice Stoughton leans over to draw Hathorne and Corwin into a whispery huddle.

With a reluctant sigh, Hathorne tells me, "Very well. You may proceed."

Chapter 27
July

Thomas

Hathorne starts right in with the worst: "Goodwidow Blevins, confess that you are a witch, and this entire experience can be set behind you. You will not go to the gallows."

"Why should I confess to being something I am not?"

This only vexes Hathorne. "Prudence Blevins, why do you comport with Satan?"

I hold my breath, waiting for her response, and waiting to see whether she'll give it gently or heave it toward them like a javelin.

"Good judges," she begins in her wavery voice, "I am a Gospel-loving woman. Up until my legs couldn't carry me, my Salem Village neighbors would see me at our meetinghouse week after week, brought there by Thomas and Grace Still-brooke of late, on their way to the Quaker meetinghouse."

Hathorne seems surprised, as I am, that she'd mention our being Quakers, but now I see this is a reasonable strategy: lay it all out on the table so they can't fling it at her later.

"You did not answer the question," Magistrate Corwin says. "It is well known that Satan preys upon the faithful and pulls them into his dark underworld. Are you a disciple of Satan, yes or no?"

"I am not."

Hathorne is undeterred. "What familiar are you in league with? A bird, a cat, a snake?"

"I am familiar with the Gospel, only that."

Corwin asks, "Will you tell us the names of others who've gone to the dark world as you have?"

"Have not! And can't."

I think of the blood-signed marks that I saw—or perhaps imagined—the frenzied night in the pasture. I say nothing.

Hathorne asks, "Prudence Blevins, have you harmed a good citizen of Salem Village, namely your accuser, Abigail Woodstock?"

"Never! Not her nor any other person. God knows I've spat a vile word now and again at a few who've done me wrong, but never have I lifted my hand to another living being." Her face reddens, her voice keeps rising, and I fear she'll explode at any moment.

I clear my throat. "Good judges, sirs, may I speak for Goodwidow Blevins?"

"If you must," says Corwin with a sigh, "but mind your tongue, I warn you."

"Yes, sir. Has the court any evidence that Goodwidow Blevins has extraordinary physical powers, as some of the convicted witches have shown, such as George Burroughs?"

All three judges set their eyes upon Pru, doubtless noting her shrunken form, her gnarled and blue-veined hands, her weathered and wrinkled face, her drooping eyelids, and the wisps of white hair sticking out of her cap.

Chief Justice Stoughton leans back. "In my judgment, in

her present form she is incapable of inflicting physical harm."

"Yet it took only a touch of her finger to relieve Abigail Woodstock of her terrible afflictions," Hathorne smugly reminds the jurors, who are growing restless.

I've been waiting for this moment. "Sirs, may I present the testimony of Miss Abigail Woodstock?"

"Is the girl here in the courtroom?" Hathorne cranes his neck to see around the crowd.

I glance around and spot Miss Patience, who shakes her head.

"No, sir, she's unable to attend today. However, I have a statement from her right here." Waving a paper with my notes from our conversation, I begin to read.

"Not good enough," says Hathorne, cutting me off. "If the witness isn't present, her testimony is worthless. Put your paper away. Better yet, rip it to shreds."

Obligingly I rip the paper in half. "I understand. So I won't reveal to the jury Miss Abigail's doubts about the reliable Touch Test you've used so impressively, sirs."

"Enough!" Magistrate Corwin shouts.

Rapid-fire: "Or that Miss Abigail says the healing touch of Goody Blevins's finger was entirely different from the hand of the specter that afflicted her."

"That will *do*, boy! You're on a very thin bridge."

"Forgive me, gentlemen. I'm just learning the rules of the courtroom. So, to move on. I have heard that some of the apparently afflicted girls recanted. They'd lied about what happened to them, or else they'd been mistaken." I must tread carefully. "I'm not suggesting that Miss Abigail lied, but is it possible, sirs, that she was mistaken about the source of her ailments? That she'd been tormented earlier by someone or something and *expected* the same to happen when Goodwidow Blevins came near her?"

The judges don't respond, but I see one juror nodding, which gives me courage to speak and to trust in Pru. "Goodwidow Blevins, has the Devil come to you and offered you wealth or strength or rewards of any kind?"

"If the Old Serpent came near me, I'd chop him to pieces and fry him in a kettle of boiling lard."

Which reminds me of Pru telling Grace and me, *I'll take my axe to your heads quick as a whistle and use you for kindling.*

"Quite descriptive," Hathorne mutters. "Just the sort of thing a person bewitched by Satan would say and *try*, only to fail abysmally."

"Sirs," I say as steadily as I can, "the defendant has testified that she's had no contact with the Devil and none with his familiars. I don't argue that Miss Abigail was sorely afflicted, nor that she truly believes that Goodwidow Blevins is the one who did her harm. But if she has been tormented by someone or something that *looks like* Prudence Blevins, might we conclude that the culprit was an apparition conjured by the Devil, and not Goodwidow Blevins herself?"

A glance toward Miss Patience tells me that she's listening intently.

"We might consider but not conclude such a thing," says Chief Justice Stoughton.

"However," says Corwin, "if she consented to the Devil's use of her likeness, then she is in his snare."

I quickly jump in: "If she *didn't* give permission for the Devil to use her likeness, sirs, would it follow that she's not responsible for whatever the Devil does with her specter?"

"Preposterous," snaps Hathorne. "Satan cannot use a specter against the will of a God-fearing soul. Clearly, this woman is a witch!"

Stoughton counters, "Spectral evidence is no evidence at all and not to be accepted in a proper court of law."

The crowd erupts into chatter, for and against Goody Pru.

"QUIET!" shouts Magistrate Hathorne. "If you cannot behave like civilized citizens, we will ask the yeomen to escort you outside."

As the noise thins into soft rumblings, I continue my argument, embarrassed that my voice has cracked as it often does these days. "But if we can consider for a moment the mere *possibility* that the Devil can use a person against her will, and has done so with Goodwidow Blevins, then we must conclude that she is not a witch but is a victim, just as the afflicted Miss Abigail is a victim."

When Goody Pru turns her head toward me, I see a faint smile on her face—though it is quickly erased when Magistrate Corwin speaks.

"Prudence Blevins, do you realize that the child who champions you so passionately was himself arrested two weeks past?"

Above the thunder of the crowd's gasps and shrill voices, someone yells, "He's a Quaker, them what don't believe in the Devil. They *are* the Devil."

Pru sways, Grace rushes to steady her, and I stand like a statue, mortified.

That day in Old Bailey court with Father, what he didn't tell me—what I learned afterward—is that four of our brethren had been hanged just weeks earlier, for the crime of being Quakers.

Chapter 28
July

Patience

I've scarcely recovered from the shock of seeing Thomas with that pretty girl—who turns out to be his sister—when our good Salem neighbors hear that my Thomas has previously been in custody for witchcraft.

Wait, he's not *my* Thomas. But whoever he belongs to, how can anyone think he's doing the Devil's work? He refuses to do violence to anyone. He wouldn't even try to throttle the brutes who stole little Dorothy away from us.

He's no servant of Satan, Thomas isn't. Maybe Prudence Blevins isn't either—if you credit what Thomas tells the judges.

I know my sister has suffered horribly. And she's been so sure—at least since Sarah Good was carted off to jail—that Goodwidow Blevins is responsible. But now Thomas makes a convincing argument that she's been mistaken.

She's improved since Goody Blevins was arrested, though. Is that because Goody Blevins is her tormentor, or because the Devil would have us *believe* she is?

It's all so confounding. I have no answers, only endless questions.

Thomas

I am still rooted to my spot. What must Miss Patience be thinking of me now?

Goody Pru shuffles closer to the judges' table, with Grace right behind her in case she should fall. Her voice now is as strong as a good wind: "Thomas Stillbrooke is a goodhearted lad, he and his sister both. They can't help it that they were born Quakers."

I'd find that amusing if I weren't so frightened for all of us—Grace, Pru, and myself.

Suddenly the crowd seems to part as Goodman Cawley strides through the throng, right up to the judges' table.

"Thomas Stillbrooke is my apprentice, and a fine cordwainer he's turning into."

"Goodman Cawley . . ." Magistrate Hathorne cautions him.

"Are you good gentlemen saying that I'd take a boy into my shop who was double-time an apprentice of the Devil? I keep the boy plenty busy. He has no time to waste on satanic nonsense."

Magistrate Corwin says, "Thank you, Goodman Cawley. You may step aside."

"Not yet. You all know who I am, where I come from, who's my kin."

I watch the jurors' eyes spark with recognition. Had Goodman Cawley not already told me that he's related to Governor Phips, all these respectful countenances might convince me that he was kin to the king himself.

"I don't know the books like you Harvard gentlemen. What I know is leather and tools and that I make the finest shoes this side of the Atlantic Ocean. So does Thomas, or he will with time. He'll know *your* business in time too. Already has a good start at the lawyering."

He turns to me just long enough to give a quick nod.

"This witchcraft business is turning Salem into hell on our shores. It's ruining lives, swallowing up time that could be put to good use with making shoes, building ships and cabinets, blowing glass, spinning wool. Honorable work, all of it. So enough of this. I'll hear no more about Thomas Stillbrooke being the Devil's plaything. Now, let's get on with what we came here for."

The judges are speechless as Goodman Cawley turns and blends into the crowd.

Finally, Chief Justice Stoughton finds his tongue. "It is my understanding that Quakers do not deny the existence of the Devil, the Great Deluder, correct?"

"Correct, sir," I say. "In my faith, as in yours, the Devil is a very real and menacing evil."

"And you do not deny the existence of witches?"

"We do not."

"That established, I believe you have something more to say about the defendant."

"Yes, sir." I shake off the clouds in my head, trying to remember what I've said already and what more I mean to say. "Your men have searched Goodwidow Blevins's humble home, and you found no poppets, no charms, no poisons, no books of conjuring, no familiars of any sort. In sum, no evidence of witchcraft."

Magistrate Hathorne interrupts. "Why then do so many townspeople, besides the poor afflicted girl, *believe* Prudence Blevins is a witch?"

Should I say what's in my mind? Take a chance, as Pru did in mentioning that Grace and I belong to the Society of Friends?

I do. "Respectfully, please consider this, if you will. The woman has been widowed more years than she was married. She has no children, no kin of any sort, and less money. When my sister and I first came to Goodwidow Blevins, she was half-starved and hissing angry as a caged dog."

"Answer the question!"

"I will, sir, but you might not like the answer. I think people of Salem say Goodwidow Blevins is a witch for two reasons. First, truthfully, she's coarse and wicked-tongued at times. She threatened to use my sister and me for kindling."

There are a few titters of laughter from the audience.

"But the real reason good and faithful people believe she's a witch is that they don't want to recognize what a poor, old, meanspirited widow needs. If they did, then they'd have to serve those needs."

No one speaks for a minute or so until Chief Justice Stoughton turns to the jury and says, "We trust that you worthy gentlemen have not been deluded by the Devil and that you can render an honest opinion."

"Yes, sir, we can," says one of the jurors. I recognize him. I've passed his blacksmith shop many times.

"Very well," concludes Chief Justice Stoughton. "Sum up for the jury, Master Stillbrooke."

"Thank you, sir." I search my memory for words that sound legal. "My argument makes three points. The first point: The defendant has firmly denied that she's guilty of witchcraft. The second point: I put it to you that the Devil has used her image against her will and without her knowledge. She has fasted and prayed to be free of this specter. Please allow in your able minds some doubt about whether spectral evidence is fitting in a court of law, but that's something to be argued some other time. For now, we've demonstrated why the Touch Test isn't enough to convict an innocent person such as Prudence Blevins."

I pause to draw breath. Silence weighs upon the room.

"My final point is this: Goodwidow Blevins is what you in your faith would call an elected saint—a faithful, God-fearing, Gospel-loving member. And to prove it, I ask you to allow one piece of evidence I know you gentlemen have used in other trials."

I wait for a response, but none comes, so I lay my hand on Pru's shoulder. "Prudence Blevins, please recite the Lord's Prayer."

"Our Father, Who art in Heaven, hallowed be Thy name . . ."

When she comes to the end of the prayer, the chief justice tilts his head toward the jury. After a flurry of whispers, the leader among the jurors makes a sign to Chief Justice Stoughton in some silent language between them. The three judges cover their mouths and confer.

At last Chief Justice Stoughton says, "Not guilty. Take her home."

Chapter 29
July

Patience

I watch Prudence Blevins leave the meetinghouse supported by the two Stillbrookes. How can I go to the market square and tell Abigail that her tormentor runs free? Well, not runs—shuffles, staggers. Is this justice? Abigail will not think so.

Still, I must admit that Thomas was brilliant. He'll not stay a shoemaker long. Am I to be the wife of a rich lawyer someday?

Banish that thought! Even if a hundred stumbling blocks were cleared away—I'm too young, he's penniless, he dislikes animals—I cannot imagine marrying a Quaker. I'd have to convert to that heretic faith myself and spend the Lord's Day in a silent meetinghouse that doesn't even have a steeple. Aside from the consequences to my immortal soul, Father would never allow it.

What's more, Thomas doesn't like me even a tiny bit. Even if the matter of religion—the only matter of importance in life!—could somehow be sorted out to both our satisfaction, a clever boy like Thomas Stillbrooke wouldn't want his children to have a mother who can scarcely read her Bible and can't write a proper sentence.

Well, I can and shall learn.

Thomas

"Flax is blooming," Pru says back at the house, bending to snap off a blue flower and toss it to the air.

"For Heaven's sake, Goody Pru, that was a lovely posey," Grace cries.

So Pru's just as quarrelsome as ever, and there hasn't been so much as a hint of gratitude for my help at the trial. Grace frowns at her now.

"I saw that," Pru snaps. "You expect me to be as jolly as a jester? I'm just as poor today as I was yesterday."

"But you're out of that dreadful jail," Grace reminds her.

And now Pru does something we've never seen in the six months we've lived with her. She grins.

"How grateful we are to Thomas, are we not, Goody Pru?" Grace prompts. "A simple thank-you would suffice."

The grin disappears. Pru snorts. "Beat out those pompous old fool judges, Thomas did."

"He did, and missed a whole day's work at the cordwainer shop," says Grace. "Well? I'm waiting."

"For what?"

"Never mind, you're not going to hear it," I mutter.

"Oh. That. Thank you, Thomas." Pru says it grudgingly, and Grace puts an arm around her, which Pru shakes off. "Don't suppose there's so much as a dried-out heel of bread in the house."

"A fresh loaf," Grace boasts.

"Anything to smear on it? Butter? Honey? Gooseberry jam?"

"No! Prudence Blevins, you're impossible," says Grace as she throws the door open on our humble shack. Home.

Patience

"Lovely mackerel, fruit of the sea," Mother sings to a small circle of goodwives. Abigail reaches into the water bucket, where we keep the handful of live fish, and waves a wriggling cod in each hand.

She searches my face for word about Goodwidow Blevins. I pray she won't be crushed to bone powder when I tell her the news.

I might as well just blurt it out, as I usually do. "The judges and jury say she's not a witch. They say you must have been afflicted by a specter that the Devil used without her knowledge."

There's a long, awkward silence while I toggle on one foot, waiting for her to explode. She plops both fish back into their water bucket. I watch the two chase each other around in the bucket, frisky as puppies, as if they understand they've been given a second chance.

"I know you're disappointed, after all the agonies you've suffered," I say, "but I truly believe that Goodwidow Blevins is not your enemy."

Emptyhanded now, she wraps her arms around her middle. "Truth be told, I—I've had doubts of it. Doubts that she was a witch. But who else had I to blame for my misery once Sarah Good was hanged? And I didn't dare recant, lest I be accused of witchcraft myself, as Mary Warren was."

My heart drops all the way to my stomach. If my sister was unsure, all this time, that Goody Pru was the Devil's servant, how many other accusers have been unsure? How many people have been mistakenly accused? How many have been unjustly killed?

I wonder . . . could all their suffering have been the work of their own minds, like a terrible nightmare that they truly believed was real? Could they all have pointed trembling fingers at an *enemy* who they thought was a witch, but who was actually a creature of their own imaginations?

These thoughts rush through my head like floodwaters. If I don't take care, I'll be driven headlong downstream.

Abigail adds quietly, "Perhaps the Devil used Goodwidow Blevins for his own evil ways. If she hurt me, I think it was not of her own free will."

"Yes! That's what Thomas said. He defended her brilliantly at the trial. You should have been there to see it."

Abigail nods slowly. "I was not there, but I *was* on Gallows Hill. I saw those women led up to their doom."

It was her choice to go, but still—she's been carrying the memory of that day ever since, knowing she had a hand in it.

"I heard her words, Sarah Good's. The minister said for all to hear that Sarah Good was a witch, and she knew full well that she was a witch, and didn't she want to confess to ease her soul? I shall never forget what she said: 'I am no more a witch than you are a wizard, and if you take away my life, God will give you blood to drink.'"

I gasp. Sarah Good never did mince words if she felt she'd been wronged. She wouldn't have hesitated to curse the whole lot of us for letting her hang at Gallows Hill.

Abigail gives me a sickly smile, such as she shows Father when he demands we mow hay under the full moon. "I'm . . . relieved that I won't have to see Goodwidow Blevins struggle up the steps to the gallows. She's . . . forgiven."

There she is—my stubborn, irritable, dramatic, *generous* sister. How can she be the same person who railed against Goody Pru for weeks? Truly, she is a puzzle to me—as I suppose I am to her.

I can't bear to dwell on the gallows any longer, so I resolve to make use of her generosity while it's in full bloom. "Abigail, will you help me to read and write proper?"

She stares at me, no doubt surprised by the turn in our conversation. "I'm slow myself when it comes to writing, but I'll give you what I know—baby words like *mama* and *run* and *cat*. Why would you want to learn all of a sudden?"

"Someday I'll be a mother and will need to teach things to my children."

"Ha! You, a mother—I can't see it. You'll be a cross old maid snarling at other people's children. Or maybe you'll be the wife of a swineherd with a houseful of suckling piglets, while I'll be married to a wealthy gentleman with servants to clean and cook and fill a tub with rosewater for my bath."

"Then I'll bring my pigs to your house."

"You will not!"

The sun is high, and Mother has peddled the next-to-last fish of the morning, a scrawny cod that poor Goodwife Dulcie examines forlornly. She'll take it home to her brood, and it'll be lucky if they get a bite each. I scoop up the one fish left, barely big enough for bait, and slide it into Goodwife Dulcie's bag while Mother's busy counting the coins in her pocket.

Abigail's smile is brighter this time. Perhaps the worst of the turmoil is over. "You're as soft as a dandelion, Patience, but I suppose that will be comforting for the piglets."

While I gather up the empty baskets and Abigail pours the water out of the bucket, I ask her, "Do you ever think about Dorothy?"

"Dorothy this, Dorothy that," sighs Mother. "It's all I hear from you, daughter. Bah." Her pockets jingle as she goes to wake Molasses and unhitch her from her favorite shade tree.

"I think of her often." There's a catch in Abigail's throat. "Will they take her to Gallows Hill, do you suppose?"

"Oh, dear Lord, I should hope not!"

"Then what's to become of her? If she's a witch . . ."

"Well, suppose she *isn't* a witch? Do you really think Satan would claim one so sweet and young? She's barely five." Even as I ask, I'm reminded of the snake that sucks the child's fingers, or so she says. "Anyway, a witch needn't stay a witch all her life."

"Perhaps not," says Abigail pensively. "Things change." Though she doesn't say it, I suspect she's thinking of the shifts in her own life through this bewildering year of bewitching.

I avoid Abigail's eyes as I toss a stack of baskets into the wagon. "So it's settled, then."

"What's settled?"

"That we'll find a way to get Dorothy freed from jail and bring her home to be our little sister."

The bucket clatters when Abigail flings it into the wagon. "You're serious?"

"I am, absolutely. Mother agrees, or nearly so. Or will soon. We just have to convince Father."

"Oh, that should be easy," Abigail mutters, heaving herself into the wagon. She settles back on a cushion of baskets, fishnets, and cloths. "As easy as convincing a rooster to give us his chin wattles."

Chapter 30
August

Thomas

"A fine friend I was," Thatcher says. He catches up with me as I hurry along Ipswich Road to the shop, with three new orders for Goodman Cawley. "I shouldn't have left you that night in the pasture."

"If you hadn't, you probably would've ended up in the Salem jail like me."

Thatch kicks a stone up the road, scampering left and right in pursuit of it. "Was it hideous? Did they beat you?"

"Yes, it was hideous, but no, they didn't beat me. Just left me to the mercy of the rats and the lice and the four sick, desperate fellows in my cell."

"Sorry, friend." The word *friend* eases me. Thatch picks up the stone and throws it as far as he can. "I had to leave the pasture. It was starting to make me barmy, you know what I mean?"

"I know. I can't describe how tempting it was when you were no longer there to keep me on an even keel. It was like . . . Imagine you've been lost in a snowstorm for hours, and up ahead is a house aglow with light, smoke pouring out of the chimney. Your feet ask no questions. They just keep taking you toward that house where warmth and relief are promised."

"You, uh, didn't knock on the door of that house, did you? Sign the Devil's book, I mean."

"I did not." Nor do I tell Thatcher about the girl with the beautiful hair. I've not seen her since. Perhaps I imagined her, or my mind transfigured her features to make her unrecognizable. "Remember you once said I was lucky not to have a father to lead me into bloody work? It was my father's voice pounding in my head that tore me away."

"Don't know if I'd've been able to resist."

"Oh, you would have," I tell him, though I'm not sure. We pass the blacksmith's shop and the glassblower's, with heat pouring out into the already stifling air. "I looked for you at Goody Pru's trial," I add. "Where've you been for the past weeks?"

"Went up to Maine, me and my pa. They're building a new meetinghouse in a town up there, and they've hired the best carpenters in New England for the task." He takes a deep, hat-sweeping bow. "We're heading back there for another few weeks till we get the place built. Leaving right after the next hanging."

"Yes, I heard Gallows Hill was going to be called upon again soon." I swallow sour juices at that thought.

"Nineteenth of August—only one woman, for a change, and four men. One of 'em's George Burroughs." Thatcher gives me a look that requires no other words. The name *George Burroughs* vibrates between us.

To be sure, we've heard nothing but ill of that man. But did we actually see his specter in the pasture with the Devil-worshippers? Or was that only what the people wished to see?

What I witnessed that night is foggy in my mind now, more illusion than reality.

Nevertheless, Burroughs will go to Gallows Hill, whether he's truly a powerful servant of Satan or not.

I have much to learn about the law.

Patience

The Stillbrookes have got Goodwidow Blevins out for a spot of sunshine, which I daresay will do her good, because her wrinkled face is as pale as goose feathers. At first Thomas doesn't see me, partially covered by a hedge of blue flax.

It's Goodwidow Blevins who spots me. "What's she doing here?"

Thomas spins around. "Miss Patience?"

I dip to a curtsy. "Could I have a word, Thomas Stillbrooke?"

With a suspicious glance at me, his sister ushers Pru away, and Thomas watches me expectantly.

Why haven't I worked out what to say? My usual impatience sent me here before I could think my words through. Stammering, I plow ahead as if through a bumpy field. "It—it's about Dorothy. I know you spoke to Magistrate Corwin about setting her free ages ago."

"Did me no good, her even less."

"Yes, but I thought you might try again with that new judge. Stoughton, is it? He seems less like a man with his feet stuck in mud."

"I doubt I'd get anywhere. It's just sheer luck that I got Goody Pru out of their clutches."

"Not sheer luck. You were brilliant!" How adorable to see him flush. "Will you try? Tell him that Dorothy will come to live with my family if she's free of that horrid dungeon. We'll be a good, Godly influence on her and raise her to reject the Devil."

His blue eyes slide side to side. I can see that he's thinking it over. "I'll try. Don't expect much."

But I expect everything! That's how much confidence I have in the shoemaker's apprentice.

Thomas

The Woodstocks are loading their wagon to leave the market when I timidly step up to the fish stall.

"Fish are gone, every last one," Goodwife Woodstock tells me curtly.

I take a deep breath. "I'm happy for your good fortune, goodwife, but I've not come to buy today. May I have a moment with Miss Patience?"

I see the woman's brow wrinkle in disapproval, especially when Patience smiles broadly. But Goodwife Woodstock nods. "Five minutes only. Molasses has stayed too long in the sun."

Miss Patience expects good news. "What is it?" she asks eagerly.

"Chief Justice Stoughton isn't entirely against releasing Dorothy."

"Then we shall go fetch her from the jail tomorrow!"

"Not quite that easy. There's a matter of money. The jail demands a ransom for her upkeep all these months. Properly it would be fifty pounds—"

"But that's a fortune!"

"Indeed, so Stoughton has had it reduced to four pounds."

"Ugh! Still more coin than my family sees in a year. *They* put innocent people in jail but charge *us* to get them out!" She spins away from me. "I have as much chance of rounding up four pounds as I have borrowing Queen Mary's underdrawers." She blushes, realizing what an impertinent thing she's just said.

Goodwife Woodstock's fishmonger voice sailing across the square saves us from the awkwardness. "Into the wagon, daughter, or you'll be walking in the heat of noon."

Miss Patience sighs and says to me, "I suppose you did your best."

Which isn't good enough.

She huffs over to the wagon where their horse patiently paws the ground, and I'm left feeling no better than an earwig.

Patience

I've waited days and days for William Good to come begging fish, and now he's here, his soul soaked in dandelion wine or rum, or both. This is my chance.

Laying on all the sweetness I can muster, I say, "Good morning, Goodman Good. I've been thinking of your precious Dorothy. I know how much you love her."

"With all me heart," he says, slapping his chest. "Who?"

"Your daughter, Dorothy." My smile is a fool's grin. "I know you'd like to free her from the terrible chains in that prison."

"I've no woman, no home to bring her to."

"She'll live with us Woodstocks."

He comes sober for a minute. "Fair, good. Oh, but they ask money, those jail thieves do, of which I've got none. Poor as porridge, I am." He struggles to work his hand into his pockets, tottering on his heels.

"Just four pounds," I say, as if it weren't a small fortune. One my own father would never consent to pay, even if I dared ask him. "And you wouldn't want to see your precious child buried in a pauper's grave, which she soon will be if nothing's done. She can't survive much longer as she lives now." I can at least appeal to his sense of decency, what little he might have.

He slaps his pockets, turns them inside out. Two pence pop out, and I catch them before they hit the ground.

"That is an excellent start, Goodman Good!"

He blinks to bring me into his vision more clearly—my hands clutched to my heart, my eyes wide—and he says, "Lemme round up what I can. Be back tomorrow."

If William Good is good at anything, it is collecting enough bits and pieces here and there to suffice for his purposes.

Now I have to bring Mother and Father along. Mother? Possible. Father? It depends on his mood—and how the fish have done. He's best after a mighty catch and with food soothing his belly.

*

The only sounds at our table are the metal spoons scraping the wooden bowls of our savory cornmeal mush. So everyone, even Ruff, jumps when my high pipe voice cracks the quiet.

"Father, I've a great favor to ask of you. It's about Dorothy Good."

Mother shakes her head, but I pretend to miss the warning.

"You know how she's been kept in jail under the most revolting conditions, filthy and starved and chained."

Father doesn't miss a bite. His spoon runs from bowl to mouth, back and forth, but on its way to the bowl for another load, he says, "You told us, daughter. I sent you to the minister on it."

"Yes, but . . ."

"And now what?" he asks tartly.

"Papa."

How startled he looks by this affectionate word! Abigail sucks her last bite of mush off her spoon and rolls her eyes toward the roof.

"The authorities are keen to release her from jail." Of course, I shall not mention the four pounds' ransom. He would never pay a hundredth of that amount. "I would like to bring her home to live with us." Before he or Mother can respond, I hurry through my plan. "She won't eat much, nor take up much space. We can make a pallet bed for her up in the loft, and she can sleep there with Abigail and me."

Mother rips a piece of bread from a crusty round loaf. "Who'll look after her? Not me, I can promise you that. I've enough to do."

"You won't need to do anything, none of you. I'll take care of her myself, except Abigail can teach her to read and write."

Abigail gapes at me but offers no protest.

Father opens his mouth to reveal a clump of mush. "No."

A dutiful daughter would fall silent and accept this answer, but I will not surrender yet. "Please, Papa? What can I say to convince you?"

Before he can shush me, Abigail comes to my aid. "Remember once during our Bible study, you read to us about how our Lord frees the captives?" Well! It seems my sister *has* changed.

"Not infant witches," Father mutters.

Mother offers him a clump of bread. To soften him up? "I believe, husband, there's something like that in Isaiah. Something about hearing the groaning of the prisoner."

"Yes!" I cry. "And bringing out prisoners doomed to death from the dark dungeon. I remember it—you taught us so well. Oh, Papa, it's the Christian thing to do!"

He returns to the rhythm of spoon-to-bowl-to-mouth. He doesn't say no again, which for Father is almost like saying yes.

Chapter 31
August

Patience

The very next day William Good comes running up to our stall, more clear-eyed and surefooted than we've seen him all year. He's carrying a bushel basket stuffed to the brim and covered in a thin blanket.

"I've got it, got it good, Woodstocks," he boasts as the basket thuds onto Mother's table. "Enough to get my poor little witch-child out of jail and situated in your blessed home." From his tattered sleeve he pulls out a scrap of paper with some words scribbled on it. "See here? Says I'm giving her to you."

Mother glares at him. "She's not a stray pup, William."

"Aw, no, she's a precious little waif. See right here? I put my mark on it, so she's yours proper and forever, 'case anybody asks."

"*I'm* asking, goodman," I cut in. "Where's the money to ransom her out of jail?"

"Well, that's the beauty of it, miss. I've been all over town encouragin' my friends—"

"Begging your fellow sots in every tavern in the Bay Colony," says Mother.

"Might've missed one or two over near Ipswich. Took up a collection, I did, every kind of money." His hand flaps around under the blanket, and he pulls out a string of shining beads that clatters to the table. "This here's wampum, made of seashells. Mate of mine got 'em trading with the Narragansetts, back-*when*. And look at this." He plunks down a large silvery coin. "Spanish piece of eight, ever see one? Comes from the West Indies. Look, here's a gold coin the size of me nostril, and this here's a handful of shillings. Must be twenty of 'em, makin' up a pound."

I sigh. "This is not enough for the ransom, Goodman Good."

"Aye, but wait till you see the rest." He throws back the blanket to reveal a thick hairy piece of *something*.

Mother recognizes it. "A goodly piece of beaver fur."

"Aye, a fine pelt! Legal tender!" Goodman William says. "Put it all together, add a few ears of corn, throw in the bushel basket, and it'll be right near four pounds' worth, don't you reckon?"

Thomas

I thought nothing on earth or in Heaven would get me back into a jail again. The smell of my cell still lingers with me weeks later. But Miss Patience has persuaded me to go with her to Ipswich to rescue Dorothy. I suspect it's to make up for my doing so little to prevent the child's capture.

When I climb into her family's wagon for the trip, she thrusts a bushel basket into my arms. "I pray this is enough to pay the ransom, if they don't count and weigh it all too closely. There's even a beaver skin in there—still has a bit of a smell. Isn't it absolutely revolting?"

This she is asking the cordwainer's apprentice, who loves all manner of leather? To me the beaver pelt smells musky and fragrant. Fish smell, now, *that's* revolting.

At the Ipswich jail, Miss Patience transfers the bushel basket from me to a guard. "Ransom for Dorothy Good, four pounds' worth. Who does it go to?"

He hefts the basket with a gleam in his eye that tells me one thing for certain: the ransom will go into his coffers, not the jail's. Another guard pulls a kerchief up over his nose, leads us down the cobblestone steps and along the oozing walls. It's hot and airless and stinks of decay.

There are fewer women in the jail now that so many have been hanged, and those who remain are too sick or too weary to petition us for anything. So the dungeon is eerily silent, and Dorothy's cell is the last one at the end of the dark, musty tunnel.

The guard throws open the cell door, unlocks the ankle iron on the child, and hastens upstairs.

Dorothy's eyes are vacant, her face flat. She flops as if she's boneless, like a doll Grace once had. Her bare feet lie unmoving on the wet, foul floor. I'll see that she gets a new pair of shoes.

"Dorothy, it's me, Patience." She wraps the child in the blanket she took off the bushel basket. Dorothy says nothing, doesn't even moan. Patience lifts the bundled child and gives her to me to carry up the steps. She's as light as a house cat. The dampness of her clothes leeches through the blanket and my topcoat.

As we walk, Miss Patience murmurs gentle words: "Dorothy, you are coming to live at my house . . . you will be my little sister . . . you will sleep next to Abigail and me . . . we will feed you fish soup, mashed corn, candied sweet potatoes . . ."

Dorothy is so still in my arms that I wonder if she's alive. The first time she moves is when the sunlight shocks her and she lifts a stick-arm to protect her eyes.

Miss Patience says, "Abigail has a tub of water in our garden waiting for you. It'll take so many changes of the water and a whole pile of washrags and strong lye soap to clean the grime off, little one, until we find the real you under it all."

The first croaky sound we hear from her is "Mama?"

Chapter 32
September

Patience

Dorothy has been with us for a few sad weeks. Each day Abigail and I gently bend and push and pull her little legs and arms to exercise limbs that haven't been put to use since March. They're as rubbery as boiled shrimp. She's not strong enough to walk alone yet—she will be soon, we'll see to it. Watching her slither across the floor on her belly, I try not to think of the snake that used to sit under her chair and suck between her fingers, or so she believed. Mercifully, it has not followed her to our house.

All her hair fell out in clumps when we washed it, leaving her as bald as a pumpkin. Now a fuzz is beginning to grow on the top of her smooth head, like a sheep after a shearing.

At first, she could barely swallow a sip of Mother's healing ginger tea. She'd entirely forgotten how to chew. I never would've thought that possible.

Words? She lost them during all those months in dark solitude. A few are coming back.

Mother says, "Give her time. She's getting stronger, and we'll soon see a bit of meat on her bones."

She has won everyone over, even Father, who prays with

her before she's put to bed each night. The only one not smitten with her is Ruff, who's jealous that Dorothy gets so much attention and he so little. Wouldn't you just know? Ruff is the one Dorothy loves best in the family. She's always had a fondness for animals, like witches do.

Thomas

The burnisher is coal-hot, and I rub the soles of Goodman Mulberry's new boots until they're shiny enough to show my reflection.

"A well-turned pair of boots," Goodman Cawley says, lowering his spectacles to the tip of his nose. "It won't take seven years to turn you into a fine cordwainer, sought after by the rich and famous all up and down the New England coast."

It's good to hear this praise. But for all the gratification this work has given me, making shoes and boots isn't what I want for my entire life. I'm promised to Master Cawley for another six years. By then I'll be twenty-one and old enough for marriage.

Father was that age when he and Mother married, and according to our tradition, they were equal partners. As Mother's foot worked the treadle of her loom, she would say, "Thomas, someday thee must choose a wife who can weave a tight, comfortable blanket."

"Is that all she need be?" I used to ask with a laugh. But Mother had a whole slew of other requirements.

"No, son—first thee must find thy way to work that gives thee pride and pleasure, as thy father has in shipbuilding. Then thee shall choose a wife who will laugh and cry with thee, who will share with thee a piece of her mind, good or ill, and who will never give thee a moment's boredom. Such a woman is worthy of being thy life's companion and partner."

True partners, my parents, though that is not the custom among our Puritan neighbors. We have so much in common yet are so far apart. In a few years I might have to go all the way to Pennsylvania to find a husband for Grace among the large Society of Friends congregation there.

As for myself? Who knows? Perhaps despite all that separates us, I'll find favor with a strong-willed girl who does *not* look like a bulldog, a girl with rich brown locks . . . but I'm in no hurry.

"Thomas, you've burnished that heel so much that it won't grip the road." Goodman Cawley hands me a file to rough up the underside of the heel. "Some weeks ago I mentioned that I need you to write me a paper, proper and legal, did I not?"

"Yes, sir, but you never mentioned it again. I thought you'd changed your mind."

"It's been in my mind at odd moments ever since that day, and now I'm set to tell you what to put on that paper."

When I've laid the file down, I take up a scrap of dried rag paper and the sharpened turkey feather quill I use for keeping Goodman Cawley's accounts. "Ready, sir."

Goodman Cawley props up his feet on the worktable and leans back, cradling his head. "It's my last will and testament you're to write."

"You're not . . . ?"

"No, I'm not standing at the edge of the grave. I'm sturdy stock, good for a few more years. But I want it known what my wishes are."

Relieved, I open the jar of ink, which is pungent and makes me sneeze.

"God bless. Now, I'll tell you what's in my mind, and you make the words all pretty and proper. When I'm too weary to work the leather, or when I'm tired of being responsible for every detail, or when I finally do leave this mortal world—whichever one of those comes first—I want my shop to keep on going. No other cordwainer will do for Salem Village. Understand?"

"Yes, sir."

"I don't see you writing much."

"Just a few words. These notes will help me remember your wishes when I make it all proper and legal."

"Ah, well and good. As I was saying, I want this shop to keep on doing what the Lord calls a master cordwainer to do. It'll need the right person to look after it. So, I am willing my shop to the right person."

There's a long pause while I hold the quill in midair and all sorts of thoughts race through my head. Who will get his shop? Am I to go along with the shop, to fill out my years as apprentice with the new owner? Goodman Cawley has no son, no heirs of any kind, and I can't imagine him leaving the shop to a stranger. Besides, who would know as well as he does the heft, the fragrance, the stretch of clean leather?

I look up at Master Cawley, who seems to be studying my face. I'm not sure if he expects me to comment—to say what I'm thinking. I glance around at the glazing iron, the knives, the benches worn smooth.

"So, Thomas, this is what I've decided. We shall change the name of the shop to Cawley and Stillbrooke."

My heart leaps—and yet still I think longingly of my law book. "I don't know what to say, Goodman Cawley."

"Say nothing. Don't embarrass yourself, for here is my intention: I shall will the shop to your sister Grace."

"What?" I shout. Hastily I calm myself so I won't look like such a fool. "A curious choice, if I may say so."

"The most logical choice. You will soon be going off to Harvard to study the law."

"I will?"

"That is your heart's desire, is it not?"

I nod but cannot answer.

"So, starting the day you leave, Miss Grace Stillbrooke will be the owner of this shop. I will continue the work here as her humble employee, but on holidays, you'll come back to Salem and run like a rabid dog to make up for the time you've neglected here. Five days' work in two. Thus, you and your sister will have an income to pay your education, and Miss Grace Stillbrooke will have a dowry so she can reel in a good, honest husband. It's a solution that suits us all. Now, go home and don't come back until you have it all pretty and proper, on fine calfskin vellum."

Patience

What a gloomy little thing Dorothy is, especially when she remembers that her mama isn't coming back, ever. We try to cheer her by softly singing psalms and telling little riddles and rhymes. Of course, we clap wildly at each of her small victories, especially her first smile. But it's all so slow, and Heaven knows, I want things—I want my whole life—to speed up.

Strange, isn't it? She hasn't asked for her father, and he's never come round. Thomas Stillbrooke has, though, bringing little gifts for Dorothy: pretty stones, a small swatch of cowskin that's smooth as paper, a bit of his sister's cranberry jam.

Today he comes with a larger box. "Miss Patience," he says with a shy nod, since Mother is right there behind me like a hawk, and he hands me a box.

"For Dorothy?"

"No, for you, from my master, Goodman Cawley. He had to guess the size."

I tear the box open and pull out a handsome pair of shoes shined to a golden glow. Though he *says* that Goodman Cawley fashioned the shoes, I shall always believe that Thomas, the shoemaker's apprentice, made these just for me.

Chapter 33
October

Patience

Now that Dorothy is walking and playing in the pumpkin patch, Ruff has forgiven her and has become her faithful friend. She is reading better than I am already. How unfair, when I'm twice her size and three times her age.

I haven't the patience to wend my way through all those blurry words that seem to jump around on the page. Words come to my tongue easily—*too* easily, Mother would say—so I have carved my way around all that balderdash by grace of an excellent memory. What's the point of memorizing dozens of psalms if you can't use them for a good end, which is to recognize their words wherever they pop up elsewhere in the Bible? I can identify troublesome words the same way you would distinguish landmarks when the ground is covered with snow.

Now, *writing* those words, that's a different matter. Whenever I practice, the pen all but leaps out of my shaky hand and lands in odd places. Once I had to retrieve it from the soup pot!

I'll wager that Thomas Stillbrooke's writing is lovely and curled and elegant . . .

Concentrate, Patience! Sitting in our pew at the meeting-house, I flip to Psalm 113: *He raiseth up the poor out of the dust and lifteth the needy out of the dunghill.* I, for one, would certainly want to be lifted out of a dunghill as quickly as possible!

Meanwhile, the sermon winds on into the second hour, and Dorothy is fast asleep between Mother and me.

"That boy over there." Mother leans over Dorothy, jerks her head toward the men's pews, and whispers from behind her prayer book. "The Cade lad, with the mop of hair down to his nose."

"Thatcher? What about him?"

"Shh!" hisses Goodwife Willowby from behind us.

Mother turns around and glowers at the goodwife. She shifts Dorothy to her lap and moves closer to me. "Your father's been talking to his father, Goodman Cade."

He who built the dreaded scaffold. Ugh!

"They're doing well for themselves, daughter. You couldn't do better, if he'll have you for a wife."

"Mother! Not Thatcher Cade!"

"Oh, I know he sows his wild oats a bit, but he'll simmer down like a pot off the fire when he has a wife and a bevy of little mouths to feed."

I think of the piglets Abigail envisioned for me.

Across the aisle, Thatcher Cade flashes a grin in my direction. Oh, mercy, did he hear what Mother said? I shall die of embarrassment right here and now, and Father can plant me in the graveyard behind the meetinghouse before dinner. Reverend Parris shall recite Psalm 25: *Remember not the sins of my youth nor my transgressions.*

On the other hand, perhaps I'll outlive my mortification and soldier onward to see what happens next. After all, I am named for one of the Heavenly virtues, so I shall look toward the future with patience, not with fear. In due time I shall find the good husband who's meant for me (mercy, not Thatcher Cade!) and more. Great things are in store for me, and don't I deserve them?

Thomas

Autumn in New England with its red and golden tree umbrellas is so much more startling than autumn in London. I leave the shop with my noon dinner, a green-stemmed red apple, yearning to see all the splendor from somewhere high above eye level.

The highest point hereabouts is Gallows Hill. So, I trudge up the hill with the apple in my pouch thudding against my leg. Last month, on the twenty-second of September, more convicted witches were hanged, seven women and one man. It was the third hanging, making nineteen people so far—as well as Goodman Corey, with the stones piled on him. You would think people's zeal for such savage spectacles would have lessened by now. And there are still accused witches languishing in jail, waiting to learn their fates—including Tituba, the first to confess all those months ago.

Just over the crest I spot a figure, probably Thatch. I hope he's here to tear down the gallows and put an end to these horrors.

Closer, I see that it's someone else. Tenting my eyes against the glare of the sun, I call out, "Sawtucket!"

"Aye, lawyer lad. What brings ye to this last-gasp spot o' ground?"

"Autumn trees. Aren't you worried someone will steal your boulder at the dock?"

"Nah, 'twas deeded to me by my father afore me, Sawtucket the First. Heard you won yer case. Got that old witch Prudence Blevins freed."

"Right, except she's not a witch. The judges even said *not guilty.*"

"Aw, that one's a witch, all right." He chuckles. "Keep watch."

"I suppose we must all keep watch, at all times, lest the Great Deluder get us in his snare." I'm remembering my night at the gathering of witches. Yet I'm also thinking of the justices and jurors of the court, who were so easily convinced that they should execute their neighbors. Every so often, it may be God's will that we trust each other, whether we've proof of one another's innocence or not.

"Heard somethin' else," adds Sawtucket.

"I expect you have," I say with a sigh.

"Heard that ye and yer lassie sister are headin' fer rich." His palm flattens, as usual, and his longest finger nearly pokes my belly.

I step away. "We're not rich yet."

The fingers fold over thin air.

"How did you find out about Goodman Cawley's will?"

"Didn't I tell ye I got my ear to the wind?"

"You don't miss a thing, do you, Sawtucket?"

He chuckles and whistles through his gapped teeth. "Fine breeze up here, all right. I come up here to sniff up the good salt air." He blows a kiss to the wind. "Hear it?"

"Hear what, Sawtucket?"

"Bend yer ear to the ground. What ye're hearin' is the crackin' of neck bones echoin' in the wind."

I don't hear it, but I know what he means, and I'm reminded of the thief boy whose fingers I broke. "It can't be right, killing twenty people."

"Can't be, and isn't, but aye, what can ye do?" He looks at me shrewdly, and I know he's telling me that I *can* do something about it. Oh, not about these twenty souls, wherever they've been sent for eternity, but about other people who are robbed of fair trials, defenders, justice.

"So, lawyer lad, somethin' else I heard. These gallows have taken all the bodies they're ever goin' to."

My fists tighten with hope. "Are you sure?"

Sawtucket gazes past me to the wooden frame of the gallows. "Sure as those trees'll give up their leaves and pile 'em on the ground afore November. That sure. But nobody knows it yet. Just yerself and me, lawyer lad." His gap-toothed smile warms my spirit as he says, "Now that ye've got that Prudence Blevins off free as turkey feathers so she won't be climbin' those scaffold steps up to the rope, and once we see a *Cawley and Stillbrooke* sign hangin' over the cordwainer's, seems like Prudence Blevins will be eatin' well. Then I might just marry that old witch!"

We both laugh, he because he's thinking of getting rich, and I because I know Prudence Blevins would make him wish he'd died single.

We fall silent, both of us, and look up toward the hallowed ground that received so many broken bodies. I breathe in the salt sea air and the breeze that's blowing the first golden leaves my way, and in my mind I see nothing but blue sky after the scaffold comes down.

Questions for Discussion

1. Patience and Thomas belong to different branches of Christianity, and each disapproves of the other's branch. What beliefs and values do they turn out to have in common?

2. How do gender roles impact the characters' lives? What unspoken rules of womanly conduct does Patience break over the course of the story?

3. Why do you think Pru takes in Thomas and Grace? What qualities do Thomas and Grace come to appreciate about her?

4. Most of the characters in this story are white people of European descent. How do they view "Indians"—Indigenous peoples of the Americas? What does this tell you about their attitudes toward people from different backgrounds and cultures?

5. Why do you think Tituba confesses to witchcraft? Why do you think Sarah Good denies the charges against her?

6. What do people claim the Devil has promised them in exchange for their service? What threats do they say he has made? What might this tell you about Puritan New England society?

7. Thomas wonders several times if the afflicted girls could be feigning their torments as a way to get attention. What do you think of this idea? What might the girls have to gain by pretending? What risks would they take by doing so?

8. How does Dorothy's arrest and treatment in jail change the way Patience sees her community? What questions does she find herself asking as she tries to help Dorothy?

9. When Thomas goes to the pasture at midnight, he has a powerful and unsettling experience, and afterward he isn't sure how much of it was real. How does it compare to the characters' experiences at the accused witches' examinations and trials?

10. How are criminal cases handled differently in 1692 Salem than they are in the United States now? Do you see any similarities?

11. According to Thomas, why is it so easy for people to believe Pru is a witch? What might motivate people in *your* community to turn against a neighbor?

12. What explanation does Abigail eventually give for accusing Pru of bewitching her—and for sticking with that accusation despite her doubts? What else do you think might have motivated Abigail to make accusations?

13. Over the course of the story, which characters defy your expectations and in what ways?

14. By the end of the story, what do Thomas and Patience expect for their futures? What do you think will happen to Thomas, Patience, Dorothy, and the other characters?

Author's Note

The seeds of this story were planted when my son David, who's a high school history teacher, gave me a book called *The Salem Witch Hunt* by an author with the intriguing name of Richard Godbeer. I blazed through his book and plunged into a quest to understand why twenty people were executed as witches in Salem, Massachusetts, during the chaotic year of 1692. Dozens of books, trial transcripts, articles, films, photos, and site visits later, I still can't grasp how it happened. But it *did* happen, so I'll share the historical facts and suggest some possible explanations.

In Europe, the late seventeenth century was a time of religious fervor before scientific enlightenment and modern medicine. England's official religion was Anglicanism, also known as the Church of England. The Bay Colonies drew settlers who practiced an offshoot of the Church of England, calling themselves Puritans. There were also pockets of minority Christian groups, Quakers and Baptists, for example. Most believed in witchcraft—both good magic and bad—and that witches were people like themselves whom Satan ensnared to carry out his evil work.

So, in January 1692, nine-year-old Betty Parris and her twelve-year-old cousin, Abigail Williams, were struck with bizarre symptoms. As an eyewitness wrote, the girls were "bitten and pinched by invisible agents . . . their limbs wracked and tormented so as might move a heart of stone." Betty's father, Reverend Samuel Parris, called for prayer and fasting. When those didn't help, he sent for Dr. William Griggs, who could find no cause for the girls' afflictions and declared them "under an evil hand," meaning they were bewitched.

The girls pointed accusing fingers at neighbors. The first named as witches were Sarah Osborne, Sarah Good, and Reverend Parris's enslaved maid, Tituba. These three endured a public hearing where they were badgered relentlessly, assumed to be guilty, and promptly jailed. Soon the afflictions—and the accusations—spread. Over the next several months, more than a hundred people in twenty-five communities were accused of witchcraft.

Servants testified against their masters, husbands against their wives, feuding neighbors against one another. In a few cases, accusers were in turn accused by others. Some people caved under pressure and confessed, even if they were innocent. Some were imprisoned for months without a trial. Several died in jail, as did Sarah Osborne and the infant daughter of Sarah Good.

Still, Salem's people made shoes, built ships, fished, and baked eel pie. Ordinary life went on, even as fourteen women and five men were brought to the gallows for public hangings between June 10 and September 22. Giles Corey refused to either confess or deny that he was a witch, so he couldn't be tried and sentenced to hang. Instead, he was pressed to death under heavy stones.

How could any of this have happened? Here are several possibilities. See which, if any, make sense to you.

- The original afflicted girls were bored, emotionally frustrated, and perhaps feeling trapped by religious and social restrictions, so they faked symptoms to gain attention, respect, and/or a sense of control over their lives.

- The community experienced a case of mass hysteria— an outbreak of unusual behaviors, thoughts, or physical symptoms that begin in the mind, not the body. It's also called collective obsessional behavior, in which one person's irrational behavior infects others. In time, many people genuinely believed they were afflicted.

- Two recent wars between colonists and the Wabanaki Nations on the Maine frontier had left refugees, such as accusers Mercy Lewis and Mercy Short, deeply vulnerable. They may have acted erratically due to what we'd recognize today as post-traumatic stress disorder (PTSD).

- Political and economic disagreements among families— and between Salem Town and Salem Village—created tensions that led to score-settling accusations.

- A poisonous fungus called ergot found its way into the flour used in bread baking, causing those who consumed it to experience nightmares, hallucinations, and convulsions.

- Religious fanaticism left no space for common sense.

- God unleashed the powers of the Devil as a punishment for the sins of mortals.

Scholars accept certain possibilities—or combinations of possibilities—more widely than others. But there are no iron-clad explanations.

Before the year ended, Salem came to its senses and stopped the accusations, trials, and executions. In May 1693, Tituba, one of the first people to be arrested, became the last to be released. Officials eventually issued compensation to some surviving families and reversed the convictions, although one woman, Elizabeth Johnson Jr., was overlooked in the pardons. Years later accuser Ann Putnam publicly apologized for her role in the deaths of innocent people. Most other participants kept quiet and tried to move on.

So, what is true in this novel and what has sprung from my imagination? I hope you'll continue reading on the subject and come to your own conclusions about what really happened in Salem, but for now, remember that this is historical *fiction*. Thomas, Grace, Goody Pru, Thatch, and Goodman Cawley are all invented. So are Patience and her family, along with a smattering of minor characters to enliven the story. However, the other afflicted people and accused witches—and the officials who condemned them—were real people.

Many scenes in the novel are based on eyewitness accounts and on transcripts of the hearings and trials. I've condensed a few events, such as the three-day examination of Tituba, to move the story along, and I've taken some creative liberties. For instance, I invented Dorothy Good's September release from jail and adoption by the fictional Woodstocks. Actually, Dorothy was jailed until December 1692, but we know almost nothing about what became of her afterward. Some accounts suggest she remained traumatized and in poverty for the rest of her life.

Here's a more heartening epilogue. Eighth graders at North Andover Middle School, near Boston, and their teacher, Carrie LaPierre, set out to clear the name of the last condemned witch whose conviction had never been reversed. After three years of lobbying the Massachusetts legislature to pardon her, they finally succeeded. In 2022, Elizabeth Johnson Jr. was officially declared innocent of witchcraft!

Yes, it came 329 years too late, but it reflects the dedication and power of young people on a mission of justice.

One question remains, though: Who on earth would want to eat eel pie?

Acknowledgments

It may be odd to thank a publisher that shall go nameless for shame-facedly canceling a contract on this book years ago when, oops, they realized they were publishing a similar novel on the same list. I'm grateful to them because that incident brought me to Carolrhoda Books, where Amy Fitzgerald, the world's finest and kindest editor, took my manuscript in hand and modeled it into a far richer and more accurate book than it would have been without her. Additional thanks to the rest of the Lerner/Carolrhoda team, including book designer Emily Harris.

I appreciate my readers, who stick with me even though I never seem to write the book they expect (as in a sequel or series). And thanks especially to my ever-patient husband, Tom, whose good nature has enabled us to travel to the places I write about. He listens endlessly, reads each story, and always declares the latest "the best thing you've ever written," which makes for a harmonious marriage!

Lois Ruby is a former librarian and the author of many books for young readers. She divides her time among family, community social action, research, writing, and visiting schools to energize young people with the ideas in books and the joys of reading. Lois lives in Cincinnati, Ohio, sharing her life and travels with her psychologist husband, Dr. Tom Ruby, and their three sons and daughters-in-law and seven obviously amazing grandchildren.